THE INCIDENTAL SPY

THE INCIDENTAL SPY

LIBBY FISCHER
HELLMANN

THE RED HERRINGS PRESS
Chicago

Copyright © 2015 Libby Fischer Hellmann.
All rights reserved.

Cover design by Miguel Ortuno
Interior design by Sue Trowbridge
Ebook produced by Stark Raving Press

ISBN: 978-1-938733-84-0
Library of Congress Case Number: 1-2334451621

For Mary Ellen Kazimer who knows the WWII era better than anyone ... including some who lived through it.

CHAPTER 1

———

December, 1942—Chicago

Lena was sure they were going to kill her when she climbed into the car. There were two of them this afternoon; usually it was only Hans. The second man sat in the back. He wasn't holding a knife or gun or even a piano wire, but there was something chilling about him. He was a beefy, muscled bull of a man, and his presence made her colder than the December day. He refused to smile, and he wouldn't acknowledge her, as if there was a limited allocation of words and gestures, and any extra would tip the scales into chaos. And Hans, who usually liked to chat, stared straight ahead, pretending to ignore her. She felt like a ghost who'd somehow slipped into the passenger seat.

Her thoughts turned to escape. She could pull the car door handle and throw herself out onto the road. She checked the speedometer. They were cruising south on Lake Shore Drive at about thirty miles per hour. She would surely perish if she did. She might be able to slide over to Hans and stomp her foot on the brake before he could stop her. But the road was icy, and the car would skid. What if it plowed into another car? She squeezed her eyes shut. She thought about smashing the window and screaming for help, but the glass of the Ford was thick, and even if she could shatter it, what would she say? Who would believe her?

She bit her lip and tried to think. Maybe she was imagining it. Maybe it was just the stress of the past six months. Or perhaps it was her time of month. Hadn't Karl always teased her about that? Karl. She blinked rapidly, trying to hold back the tears that still threatened at the thought of him.

It had been a routine day of typing and filing, much like all the others. She'd had lunch with Sonia, who poured her heart out about her husband who'd been drafted and had fought the

Battle of Midway last summer. Walking back from the cafeteria, Lena spotted the signal, a small American flag stuck in the snow-covered urn beside the 57th Street florist's shop. That meant she was to meet Hans as soon as possible.

She considered ignoring it. Just not showing up. But Max was at home with Mrs. McNulty, their upstairs neighbor and baby-sitter. She would give him supper and make sure he went to sleep if Lena had to "work late" as she explained whenever there was a meet. And a few days ago she'd let Hans know she knew. She couldn't risk not meeting him. What if they retaliated against Max?

She leaned back against the seat of the Ford and swallowed. She should have run the moment she spotted the flag, scooped up Max, and boarded the first train out of Chicago. Now it was too late. She was a fool.

The Ford slowed and turned into one of the beaches off South Lake Shore Drive. Then it slowed even more. The man in the seat behind her leaned forward. She knew what was coming. She braced herself and whispered the *Sh'ma*.

CHAPTER 2

May, 1935—Berlin

Lena headed west on *Ebertstrasse* towards the *Tiergarten* and ducked into the park. It was the middle of May, but the hot sun felt more like July. Once inside the greenery, though, the temperature cooled. A breeze swished through the trees, and birds chirped, a bit frantically, Lena thought, as though they were as disturbed as she. She rounded the corner, narrowly missing a couple of girls on bicycles, braids swinging in their wake, and caught sight of several children splashing water at each other behind the rhododendrons. Josef should be waiting for her at the statue of the woman with her hand on her breast whose name she could never remember.

There he was! With his wavy blond hair, sharp edge to his chin, and gorgeous green eyes, he looked Aryan, not Jewish. She, on the other hand, with her thick chestnut hair, brown eyes, and nose she thought was too big, but which Josef said he loved anyway, couldn't even try to pass. Josef claimed his looks had saved him from more than a few schoolyard brawls. His family had moved from Alsace years earlier, so he'd been French, German, and everything in between, he joked. But always in love with her, he would quickly add.

When he spotted her, he smiled broadly and opened his arms. She ran into them. He was the one for her; she'd known since they were five and she lent him a few coins at synagogue every week for *tzedukah*. But he hadn't realized it until a year ago when they both turned sixteen. Now they were inseparable.

Lena pulled back and studied his face. She knew she wasn't smiling, and his smile, so bright a moment ago, faded. She felt her face crumple; she couldn't keep it in anymore. Tears brimmed and trickled down her cheek.

Josef clasped her to him. "My Lena, what is wrong? Stop. All is good. We are together."

That made her cry harder.

His expression turned grim. "What? What is it?"

"Oh Josef..." A strangled sob escaped.

He led her to a wrought iron bench and made her sit. He sat beside her and grabbed her hand. Usually, the aroma of damp earth and blooming lilacs in the park made her smile, but the tears continued to stream. She tried to wipe them away with the back of her hand.

Josef brushed his fingers across her cheek. "What is wrong? You look like you've lost your best friend."

"I have," she cried.

"What are you talking about?"

She took a breath and tried to compose herself. "My parents are sending me to America. In three weeks."

Disbelief flickered across his face. "But—but your parents are planning to go to Budapest. With mine."

Lena felt her lips quiver. "*They* are. But they claim Hungary is not safe enough for me. They want me far away."

Josef fell silent.

"I tried to convince them to change their minds, but we have a second cousin, sort of an aunt, in Chicago who has agreed to sponsor me. It has been arranged."

"No." Josef squeezed her hand. It was just one word, but it said everything.

"I—I don't know what to do, Josef. I can't leave you."

He nodded. "Nor I you."

She brightened for a moment. "Perhaps you could come with me."

He turned to her. "How? You know it's not possible. I would need a sponsor, and it's not so easy for us to—"

"I can ask my aunt."

"My parents would never permit it."

She cast her eyes down and whispered. "I know. But we can't stay here. We can no longer go to school. My father lost his job at the newspaper. Your father lost his government post. It will only get worse."

Josef didn't say anything for a moment. "Let me think. I will come up with something." He pulled her close and tipped up her chin with his hand. "I love you Lena Bentheim. I always will."

"And I love you, Josef Meyer. Forever."

"Until death do us part." He leaned in and kissed her.

CHAPTER 3

1935—Chicago

But Josef didn't come up with a plan, and three weeks later, Lena boarded a ship for New York. It was a rough voyage, and she spent most of it below deck, green and seasick. She vowed never to travel by sea again. Once in New York she passed through immigration, then followed the instructions in her aunt's letter and took a train bound for Chicago.

Her "aunt" Ursula met her at the station. A thin, wiry brunette with pale blue eyes, Ursula had married Reinhard Steiner, a math professor originally from Regensburg. They'd come to the

Midwest five years earlier, when Reinhard was offered a position at the University of Chicago. Now, as they drove by taxi to a spacious, leafy neighborhood called Hyde Park, Lena found Ursula brisk and all business, but not unkind. Clearly, she had been making plans.

"... English lessons..." she was saying. "Typing, too, so you can get a job. We will lend you the money, of course, and you can pay us back bit by bit when you are employed. And Reinhard has connections at the University, so we might be able to place you there after you're qualified. The weakness in the economy still lingers, so you will be lucky to get any job at all."

Lena thanked her and gazed out the window. True, she was sixteen, an age at which many German girls left school to work or marry, but she had somehow expected—no, hoped—she would have a year or so left to study for her baccalaureate. It wasn't that she didn't want to join the adult world. It was just too soon. Three weeks ago she and Josef were in the Tiergarten stealing kisses. Now, her childhood was over. She blinked back tears.

* * *

The next six months were filled with English tutors, secretarial school, and letters from home. Josef wrote regularly, telling her about his days—he was studying at home, learning how to cook, taking long walks. He missed her terribly, he declared, and would never stop loving her. Her parents wrote cheerful letters too, never mentioning how they were coping with Hitler's restrictions. Lena knew her mother was trying to make life sound normal so Lena wouldn't worry. But the more cheerful the letter, the worse Lena knew things were. She read the newspapers. She wrote back, begging them to leave Berlin for Budapest, Paris, or New York. But leaving Germany was never mentioned, at least in the letters that came back.

Starting around the High Holidays, letters from Germany became less frequent. Then, in December a letter came from Josef.

You are lucky you got out when you did. Things here are very bad. My parents have decided to go to Budapest. I don't know how much you know in America, but in September Hitler passed the Nuremburg Race Laws. These laws strip all German Jews of their citizenship. We are now "subjects" in Hitler's Reich. The laws also forbid Jews to marry or have relations with Aryans or to hire

Aryan women as household help. They also presume to define how much Jewish blood makes one fully Jewish.

So, now everyone is arguing whether someone is a full Jew or part Jew. What does it matter? My father says if we stay we will be killed—they are considering even harsher laws. We will be nothing more than criminals. It is hard to believe.

Friends of my parents in Budapest have arranged for an apartment for us, but apparently it is quite small. We will leave in a few days. I miss you desperately. I have not seen your parents. Perhaps they have already left?

The next day a letter came from her mother. Unlike Josef's, it was strangely devoid of news. Just the same trivia her mother always wrote. Lena immediately replied asking why they hadn't left. Had they talked to Josef? Again she begged them to leave Berlin. And then she cried.

She never got a response.

CHAPTER 4

———

May, 1936—Chicago

It was exactly a year later when Ursula declared her fit to be hired. "I was a secretary myself before we came to America, you know. That's how I met Reinhard. So I know all the tricks a lazy girl does to pass herself off as competent."

Lena didn't know whether that was directed at her, but when her aunt smiled, relief washed over her. She had learned English easily; within four months she was practically speaking like a native.

"Reinhard has already talked to people at the University. The physics department is looking for a secretary. And…" Ursula's smile broadened,

"...there are two German students in the department whose English is not so good. They are thrilled at having a secretary who is bilingual. Especially in today's world," she added.

Lena swallowed. "But I know nothing about physics, Aunt Ursula. In Gymnasium I got most of the fundamental concepts wrong. Acceleration, rate, gravity... I'm hopeless."

Ursula waved a dismissive hand. "You don't need to know physics. I could barely add two and two and look where I ended up."

But Lena didn't want to meet and marry a German academician, like her aunt. Josef was waiting for her in Budapest, and as soon as she could, she would bring him to the States. In the meantime, though, she took the position.

* * *

Ryerson Physical Laboratory, a pleasant, ivy-covered building on 58th Street edged one side of the university quad. Lena liked to walk through it on her way to work, imagining she was a student at the university. She wondered if she would ever reclaim those carefree days.

Although the department was small, it prided

itself on two Nobel Prizes won by its scientists, one of whom, Arthur Compton, was the department chair. She quickly learned that Ursula was right about one thing. She didn't need to know anything about physics.

The one imperative was to make sure her typing was accurate. Most of the documents contained columns of symbols and fractions and percentages that, while a mystery to her, were known to the scientists, so it was critical to get them right. When she asked why, Professor Compton explained that the department's mission was to instill the habit of careful, intelligent observation of the external world.

"In order to do that," he said, fingering the small mustache that looked a little too much like Hitler's, Lena thought, "we expect our graduate students to replicate classical experiments by eminent investigators. And that includes the data they observe and analyze."

Lena nodded. She was intimidated by Compton but more relaxed around the students, who told her Compton's nickname was "Holly." But they never explained why, and she never figured it out. She and the scientists chatted and laughed and traded jokes that were surprisingly funny. There were the two German graduate students who had come to America a year earlier and soon depended on her to help write their papers. A young Brit and three Americans also hung around.

"There are actually three of us Germans," Franz told her one day. "But Karl is at Columbia University in New York for the semester."

"Why?" Lena asked.

The second German, Heinrich, smiled. "That's where the action is. They're doing lots of exciting experiments on the atom. I can't wait for him to come back and tell us everything."

Thankfully, Lena knew what an atom was. "But why are they experimenting with the atom?"

"Splitting it," Franz said. "Even Einstein thinks it might be possible."

"To what end?"

"Who knows? But they say Hitler is doing the same thing. So, of course, the Americans must too..." his voice trailed off. "At any rate, Karl will be back in September."

CHAPTER 5

September, 1936—Chicago

By fall Josef's letters were less frequent. He was fine, he said in the one letter she received. His mother was sick. When she coughed, her handkerchief was tinged with blood, and they feared it was tuberculosis. But he was working with a carpenter in Budapest and learning a trade. "Think how useful that will be when we build our house."

She wanted to share his optimism, but she hadn't heard from her parents in months, and Josef said he hadn't seen them in Budapest. The émigré German Jewish community there was small;

everyone knew each other. She had heard the rumors about the SS rounding up Jews and sending them to forced labor camps. She prayed that wasn't the case and that she would soon receive a joyful letter from Paris or London or Amsterdam.

She was in the filing room one afternoon, in reality just a cramped closet, when a male voice called out from the front.

"Halloo. Is anyone there?" It was a tentative voice, speaking heavily accented English that sounded like a German national. Bavarian, actually. Lena had learned how to figure out what part of Germany someone was from by the way they spoke English.

She hurried out. A young man with dark curly hair and glasses that magnified his brown eyes leaned against a wall. He was about six feet—she was using feet and inches in her calculations now—and solidly built.

"How can I help you?" she said, knowing her own accent marked her as a foreigner.

His face lit. "You are German!" Something about his expression, so innocent and yet full of delight, instantly put her at ease.

She nodded. "And you are from Bavaria."

He switched to German "How did you know?"

She tapped her lips. "I hear it."

He smiled back. "You have a good ear." He raised his palm. "Munich."

"Berlin." She did the same.

"Do you work here?"

"I am the department secretary. Since last May." She tilted her head. "Are you new?"

He laughed. "No. But I have been away."

"Oh. You are Karl."

He brightened even more. "Yes."

"You have been at Columbia in New York."

He nodded. "And you?"

She held up her hand. "As I said, I am not a student."

"Your name." There was a softness in his voice as he said it.

She felt a flush creep across her face. "Of course. Lena Bentheim."

He offered his hand. "Karl Stern."

She took it. Stern could be a Jewish name. They stood with their hands clasped a beat too long. Neither appeared to mind.

* * *

Karl came to the Physics office with a different reason every day. He needed a book from the library—she often checked them out for the students. He needed to find a paper someone else had written. He lost his schedule of classes for the fall. Lena never said anything, but she looked forward to his visits.

Two weeks later he mustered up the courage to ask her to tea.

"Tea? How—lovely." She giggled. "But we are not in London."

"Yes, of course." He flushed from the neck up. "Coffee, then."

She cocked her head. "Not in Vienna either, although it is true that Americans are in love with their coffee."

Karl's face turned crimson. He stammered. "Well—well then, I apologize for—for... " His voice faded and he seemed to shrink into himself.

"But beer," Lena smiled. "Now that's another matter. Do you think we might find a nearby tavern?"

Karl's face glowed.

"Come back at five, yah?" She said.

He nodded enthusiastically.

Lena took him to a restaurant just off campus. The menu boasted the Budweiser logo, and the words "Makes Good Food Taste Better" at the top. The tavern offered thick soups, meat loaf, and even hamburgers at prices students could afford. All washed down with beer. The pleasant smell of grease drifted through the air; Lena's mouth watered. They both ordered the meat loaf.

They talked about everything, but focused on what was happening in Germany. The Berlin Olympic Games had just ended, and Hitler had taken a keen interest, hoping his Aryan athletes would dominate the competitions. It was the irony of ironies that Jessie Owens, a Negro from America, won practically all his events. Because of the games, moreover the German government had temporarily refrained from actions against Jews.

"But more restrictions are on the way," Karl said.

Lena sat back. "Are you Jewish?"

"Of course. I thought you knew."

She leaned against the back of her chair. A deep wave of relief passed through her. Karl understood. The other German graduate students were sympathetic, but they weren't Jewish. It wasn't the same. For the first time since she'd come to America she realized how guarded she'd been.

"Where are your parents?" she asked. "And the rest of your family?"

"In Austria. I am trying to get them here. I think it will happen, but I don't know when. The U.S. has become quite restrictive about who can get in." He paused. "What about yours?"

She hesitated, then shook her head. "I don't know."

He reached across the table and squeezed her hand.

CHAPTER 6

———

By the end of the year Lena and Karl were a couple. She spent more time at his apartment, a shabby room in the southern part of Hyde Park, than Ursula's, but Ursula didn't seem to mind. It was as if her aunt knew what was happening and tacitly approved. Karl was invited to *Shabbos* dinner every Friday; it became the only big meal they ate, except when they went out.

The night she and Karl made love for the first time, she had the feeling she was his first. Afterwards she knew she had to write Josef. At first she had been wracked with guilt, and tried to keep Karl at a distance. But he was so unassuming, gentle, and smart she soon developed feelings for him. There had been no letter from Josef in months, anyway. Memories of him were fading like dried flowers inside a book, a book that had been written centuries earlier.

Meanwhile the Physics Department was suffused with an enthusiasm that hadn't been present before. Compton, the head of the department, was known for studying cosmic rays, but the experiments that intrigued the students were those Enrico Fermi started in 1934 in Europe.

One night, after they made love, Karl tried to explain Fermi's work in a way Lena could understand. "It has to do with bombarding elements with neutrons instead of protons. One of the elements Fermi uses is uranium, which is one of the heaviest of the known elements."

"Why is that important?" Lena asked.

"Because the result turned out to be lighter than the elements he'd started with."

She frowned. "What do you mean?"

"Fermi himself didn't really understand why, but others were quick to link it to Einstein's theory of $E=mc2$."

"Why?"

Karl grinned. "Because a great deal of energy was released during the bombardment." He paused. "When we figure out exactly how it happened and what exactly was released, a new world of possibilities will emerge."

Lena loved to listen to Karl. She barely understood what he was talking about, but his eagerness and love of learning kindled a desire in her to go back to school. To finish what they called, in the States, high school. Maybe, afterwards, she would even enroll at the university.

CHAPTER 7

_____

1937-1938—Chicago

The day Lena and Karl married was a warm, breezy day in June, 1937. The tiny wedding at KAM Isaiah Israel synagogue in Hyde Park included less than a dozen guests: Ursula and Reinhard, the graduate students in the Physics Department, a secretary, Bonnie, from the Math Department with whom Lena was friends, and Professor Compton and his wife. Lena had bought a white dress on sale at Marshall Field's, and Bonnie had helped her make a veil. But what she loved most were her white sandals with rhinestone bows, which sparkled in the light, making her feel as though she was floating above the ground.

After the ceremony, Ursula and Reinhard invited everyone to their house for wedding cake and champagne. Ursula surprised Lena with a marzipan cake from Lutz's, the German bakery; her aunt had gone all the way to the North side to pick it up. Later that evening, Karl's friends took them to a special performance of the Benny Goodman Trio at the Congress Hotel, and they kicked up their heels until the wee hours. Lena couldn't have asked for a more perfect day. If only her parents had been there to see it.

* * *

A few months later, as they walked to the quad from their apartment near 57th and Dorchester, Lena—now Mrs. Stern—held up her hand, watching her wedding ring flash this way and that in the morning sun. She did that a lot now. To most people, it was just a modest gold band, but to her it was as valuable as the whole of the recently built Fort Knox.

She turned to her husband. "Thank you, Karl."

"For what?"

"For everything. You made me whole again. I finally belong."

He smiled and reached for her hand. They walked a few steps in silence. Then, "I have a confession to make," she said.

"What, my darling?"

"I wish..." she hesitated. "Sometimes I just want to forget what's going on in Europe. I just want to think about our life here. Does that make me a terrible person?"

He squeezed her hand. "I do not think so. I do it as well sometimes."

"Doesn't it make you feel guilty?"

"I don't let it. And, I take heart that I am working in a field that could end the suffering there."

"But that's so far in the future... and so unsure, given how powerful the Nazis have become."

He took her arm. "Perhaps. Perhaps not. And, don't forget, Lena my darling, you are helping, too."

"I'm not doing anything except typing and filing and writing letters."

He touched her lips with his index finger. "Don't say that. Your work allows us to concentrate on our research. And that research might well give

America a valuable tool one day." He leaned over and kissed her. Lena wanted to collect moments like this, if only to store them in life's album of happy times.

So Lena tried to ignore the steady drip of bad news from Europe. It worked for a while, but like a leaky faucet, the bad news was unrelenting. Hungary was pressured to join the Axis; reportedly, Jews outside Budapest were being rounded up. Lena prayed that Josef stayed safe. She wouldn't let herself think about her parents, trying to persuade herself that whether they were at a labor camp, or had been sent to what were now called concentration camps, she was in America, and America was interested in America, not Europe.

America was focused on rebuilding its economy and staying out of the war. Of course, people like Henry Ford disparaged Jews, as did Father Coughlin, a Catholic priest whose weekly radio program drew millions of listeners. She would turn off the radio when his show began.

* * *

In March 1938, the Nazis overran Austria and

annexed it to Germany. By October they had invaded the Sudetenland, and November brought *Krystallnacht*. It was no longer possible to ignore what was happening. Europe was an ugly carcass filled with violence and death.

But the physics community of which she was now a part celebrated good news. Enrico Fermi was awarded the 1938 Nobel Prize for his work in neutron bombardment, and that made everyone optimistic about the future of nuclear research.

By December Lena had missed a period, and her breasts had grown tender. She knew from repeated discussions with Bonnie that she was pregnant. She wasn't sure how Karl would take it—he had been working such long hours—so she surprised him one evening and took him to the restaurant with the Budweiser menu. It had become their "spot."

"I have news," she said after they'd ordered beers.

Karl cocked his head. "About your parents?"

She shook her head. "No. Nothing like that."

His brow furrowed. "Then what?"

She reached for his hand. "We're going to have a baby."

Karl blinked as if he hadn't understood.

"You. And me. We're going to have a child."

A glorious smile unfolded across his face.

* * *

Just before Christmas, two scientists announced they had replicated Fermi's experiments. They had bombarded uranium atoms that threw off neutrons and energy. Under the right circumstances, they claimed, these "boiled off" neutrons might collide with other atoms in a chain reaction and release even more neutrons and energy. They called it "fission."

The scientists were from Berlin.

CHAPTER 8

1939—Chicago

In March of 1939 Hitler seized Czechoslovakia. Neville Chamberlain spoke of appeasement, and so many people wanted to believe him that the voices begging the world to stop Hitler went unheard.

A month later Karl came home, a wide grin on his face. Lena was simmering bean soup. Thick, the way he liked it.

"You look like that cat in Alice in Wonderland."

"You'll never believe it!" he said.

"What? What is it?"

"I've just had a letter from my parents."

Her eyes widened. Letters from loved ones in Nazi-occupied countries were rare. "And?"

"Next month they will board a ship in Hamburg and sail to Cuba!"

Her mouth fell open. "Really?"

He nodded eagerly. "The ship will carry almost one thousand Jewish refugees. They will stay in Havana for a while, and after that—"

She cut him off. "We can bring them here!" She waved the wooden spoon she'd been using to stir the soup. "How wonderful!"

"They say to expect a telegram from Havana toward the end of May."

"Karl. We must celebrate."

"Yes." His soft brown eyes were shining. "I think rum. Do we have any?"

She giggled. "No, but I will go out and get some. This is wonderful news."

"They will love you."

She gave him a shy smile. He hugged her, then patted her stomach, which, at six months, was nicely rounded. "And when the baby comes—"

Lena cut in again. "What's the name of this magic ship?"

"The St. Louis."

* * *

The ship sailed from Hamburg on May thirteenth. Lena and Karl made preparations. They decided his parents would take their bedroom until they found their own place. Karl and Lena would sleep in the living room. They bought a used couch, which opened into a bed. Lena planned menus for two weeks and brought home grocery bags stuffed with food.

The ship was due to land in Havana on May 27th. But the day passed with no telegram from Karl's parents. When there was still no word by evening the next day, they began to worry.

The story didn't take long to emerge. Once the ship entered Cuban waters, Cuba's pro-Fascist president, Federico Laredo Bru, decided to ignore the refugees' documents. Only twenty-two of one thousand Jews were allowed to enter Cuba. The rest were forced to stay on the ship. The refugees appealed to America to let them in, and a chorus of voices on both sides of the issue joined in. There were marches, hundreds of letters written to FDR, poignant stories about the refugees on the ship.

There were also those who demanded the ship

and its cargo be turned away. Negotiations between Cuba, the US, and even the Dominican Republic seesawed with good news one day, bad news the next. It seemed as if the entire world was holding its breath.

Ultimately, the nay-sayers prevailed. On June seventh, negotiations failed, and the St. Louis was forced to return to Europe. Lena and Karl were devastated. Karl sank into such a severe depression Lena worried he might do something crazy. She hid the kitchen knives in the back of the cabinet.

Several European countries eventually took in some the refugees, but those who went to Belgium, France, or the Netherlands were trapped when Hitler invaded those countries a year later. A few months after the ship returned to Europe, Karl got a letter from his parents. They had settled in France. That was the last time he heard from them.

* * *

At the beginning of August, Albert Einstein wrote a letter to FDR. In it, he summarized the latest scientific thinking on chain reactions, uranium, and fission. Then he wrote:

"This new phenomenon would also lead to the

construction of bombs, and it is conceivable—though much less certain—that extremely powerful bombs of this type may thus be constructed."

On September first, Hitler invaded Poland. Two days later England and France declared war against Germany.

CHAPTER 9

1939-41—Chicago

Max Stern was born two days later on September 5, 1939. Lena had an easy labor: her water broke at noon; by seven, Max made his appearance. He was a perfect baby boy: dark hair and lots of it, a lusty cry, and a determined chin that said he would not be ignored. They named him after Lena's father Maxmillian—who, if not already dead, was clearly lost to Lena.

Lena took her time recovering, so Karl organized the *bris*. He found the *Mohel*, invited the guests, ordered trays of food. Lena spent the entire time in the bedroom with Ursula. The baby gave a sharp cry when the *Mohel's* scalpel sliced his foreskin. Lena ran to the bathroom and threw up.

Max was the most adored baby ever. Lena thought of him as a little prince and, of course, quit her job to take care of him. She was determined to become the mother he deserved. After all, his birth was proof that the Nazis, no matter what, had not prevailed. It was her job to make sure it stayed that way.

Over the next year she carefully washed his diapers and bottles, made sure he had plenty of fresh air, sang and talked to him constantly. The experts said the more you talked to your baby, the smarter he would be.

Still, in the dark hours of the night, she was beset with fear. A mere sniffle meant a rush to the doctor. She worried whether she was feeding him enough. Whether he was sleeping too much or too little. Even a diaper rash made her nervous. In the deepest, darkest part of her brain she was sure that one mistake, one careless error on her part, would mean the end. Karl, who had bounced back from his depression over the St. Louis, tried to comfort her, but her outlook, so broad before, shrank into a tiny world view of what Max needed, what Max did, how Max fared. His powdery baby smell was the most seductive aroma she could imagine.

Max was asleep one summer night in July, 1940, when Karl got home. Lena usually tried to keep Max up to see his father, but tonight his little head drooped, his eyes closed, and she had to put him to bed. It didn't help that Karl was often late now that research on chain reactions and uranium compounds had picked up.

Much of the new work, he told her, was done in Berkeley, New York, and Britain, but Compton was the head of National Science Academy, and his opinion was sought on everything dealing with nuclear research. That meant lots of staff papers, analyses, and theoretical discussions that lasted until the middle of the night.

Lena had climbed into bed herself and was nodding off when Karl came into the bedroom. She could smell his beery breath across the room. Karl rarely drank. She decided to ignore him, but when he stumbled over his shoes and let out a yelp, she switched on a lamp and rose up on her elbows.

"Are you all right, darling?"

"Yah, yah," he replied.

"You're drunk."

"Quite possibly." He let out a loud burp as if to prove the point.

Lena shook her head in mock annoyance. She couldn't be angry with Karl.

"It was a crazy day. Some of us went out for a few beers to calm down."

Lena pushed herself to a sitting position. If Karl needed a few beers to calm down, this was important. "Why don't I make you some coffee?"

"Thank you, *liebchen*."

Ten minutes later, she brought a steaming cup into the bedroom, handed it to her husband, and got back into bed. She watched as he took a few cautious sips. A few minutes passed. Karl's furrowed brow smoothed out, and he looked calmer.

"So," she said. "What happened?"

He sat on the edge of the bed. "I will tell you. But first, you must take an oath that you will never repeat any of this to anyone."

"Of course," she said. "Remember, I used to work there."

He nodded. "I remember. Did you ever meet an Army officer, Colonel Charles Collins? He came to the Department often once the government created the Uranium Committee." Karl fingered the sheet Lena had draped around herself, as if he could feel Lena's skin through it. "He always demanded to meet with Compton privately. As if he was in charge and Compton worked for him."

"I don't recall him. Was he a scientist?"

"Not really. He took a course or two in college, Compton said, but he thought he knew it all."

"Just like an officer. They put on a uniform and think they rule the world," Lena said. "They are the same the world over. Why did Compton put up with him?"

"I wondered the same thing. It turns out he didn't." Karl smiled.

"How do you mean?"

"So." Karl grabbed his coffee and took another sip. "I don't know if I told you, but in May—well, this gets rather complicated—the Germans seized one of the largest heavy water production plants. It's in Norway."

"Heavy water?"

"It's a type of water that can help build nuclear weapons. It showed the world that Germany is serious about producing an atomic weapon."

Lena nodded.

"Things at work accelerated quickly after that. The Brits and the Americans do not want to fall behind, you see."

A flash of irritation washed over her. "Yes, but what does this have to do with you getting drunk?"

"I'm getting to that." He dropped his knee and ran his hand down the sheet that covered her, stopped at her breast, and cupped it. She was still nursing Max, and her breasts were heavy and full.

She flicked his hand away. "Well?"

He sighed. "Well, last month the government reorganized its nuclear research program. They're looking into several different ways to separate isotopes and produce a chain reaction. But the key is that military representatives will no longer be on the committee." He paused. "So when Collins came in today he was told he had no further reason to come into the department." Karl grinned.

"And?"

"The Colonel was not happy."

"I don't understand. What does it mean, no more military on the committee?"

"In practice, it does not mean much. It's just so that we can get enough funds to focus on the science without depending on the military for budget approval. But clearly, they will not be excluded for long. Whatever we come up with, they're going to implement."

"But Collins wasn't satisfied?"

"What do the Americans say? Not for a 'New York minute'? He became belligerent, started to make threats, said he would go to the top to complain. That the military *should* be in charge of us."

"With him as leader, no doubt," Lena said.

Karl nodded. "Of course. Then he stomped out."

Lena mulled it over. "My goodness. Such excitement!"

"At any rate, Compton stayed in his office for a while. Then he came out and gave us a stern lecture on confidentiality. He said it was vital that no one know anything about our work. Including our families. That everything we do is a matter of the utmost national security. To be held in the strictest secrecy." Karl bit his lip. "If he finds out I told you this much, he will fire me."

"I will tell no one. You know that."

"Yah, I know." He caressed her cheek. "So, that's why we went drinking. We were all a bit—how do they say in English—shaky. Suddenly, we are not at all sure what the future holds."

Lena slipped her arms around her husband. "Don't worry. I will not pry any secrets out of you. Now come to bed."

CHAPTER 10

1941—Chicago

By the time Max was eighteen months, Lena did something she should have done years earlier. One night in March, 1941, she wrote to Josef. She had no idea if he was still at the Budapest address she had for him, but she told him about Karl, Max, her life in America, and the Physics Department. She apologized for not writing sooner. She didn't know how to explain. Their love had made sense during the traumatic years in Berlin. He had been her lighthouse; the beacon of her hope. But she had moved on. She didn't say that in the letter; she simply said she hoped he could forgive her. She didn't expect him to respond, but she felt better for writing.

To her surprise, a month later she received a reply. Josef was still in Budapest. His mother had passed and his father was frail, but he wanted her to know he understood. "Time releases no one," he said. "Life always changes."

In fact, he was seeing a woman himself, and the letter Lena had written he took as a reprieve. He intended to ask this woman to marry him. He wished Lena nothing but the best for her and her family. Lena's eyes filled as she read the letter. At the same time, her guilt lifted. She felt lighter than she had in years.

As spring advanced into summer, Max was starting to talk, and his conversations, peppered with real words as well as baby talk, were a delight. Lena chatted with him most of the day, and both Lena and Karl were convinced he was an intellectual giant.

One afternoon, on a beautiful summer day that reminded her of the day they were married—it was hard to believe it had been four years already—she wheeled Max in a new-fangled baby stroller to a park adjacent to South Lake Shore Drive. Now that the North and South legs of the Drive were connected, it was busier than ever, and they crossed the street carefully. Lena meandered down to the beach at 59th Street and spread a blanket over the sand. She and Max spent the afternoon building sand castles and dipping their toes in the frigid water.

When it was time for Max's nap, she put him down on the blanket and lay down beside him. She must have dozed off too, because the next thing Lena remembered, the sun was peeking through the trees from the west. She checked her watch; they had been asleep two hours.

Hurriedly, she roused Max. He wanted to go back to the water. She clutched his hand and made one more trip to the edge of the lake, then settled him in the stroller for the journey back home.

As she made her way from the beach back to 57th Street, Lena had the sense she was being followed. She whipped around but didn't see anyone. She frowned. Max chattered away; she had to focus on him. She kept going. Once they'd crossed 57th Street to the sidewalk, the feeling intensified. She spun around again. This time she caught the shadow of a figure melting into the narrow space between two buildings. Someone *was* following them.

But who? Hyde Park was one of the safest neighborhoods in Chicago. She began rolling Max's stroller so quickly that Max started to fret. She tried to shush him, explaining they had slept so long they were late getting dinner. Max seemed to understand, because he stopped crying.

The feeling faded as she passed the shops of Hyde Park, but she was still wary. She kept looking around; no one seemed interested in her. She forced herself to stop in at the butcher's for a veal roast. Then she bought small potatoes and fresh green beans at the market two doors down. At the last moment, she added ripe tomatoes.

Back home she locked the door, something she rarely did and turned on the radio. It was filled with war news, none of it good. She started preparing dinner, wondering who had been following her and why. She was certain it was a man; she'd seen a flash of dark pants and a striped shirt.

When Karl got home, she told him.

Karl frowned. "You have no idea who it was?"

She shook her head.

He looked like he was seriously thinking. Then he looked up. "Are you sure?"

She shot him an irritated glance. "Of course. Do you think I would make this up?"

"No. But I cannot believe it was intentional. Perhaps it was a hobo who wanted your money."

She shook her head. "He did not make a move toward my wallet."

"In that case, I have no idea, *liebchen*. Maybe forget it. It might have been..." Karl shrugged... "A prank? A mistake?"

"And if it happens again?"

"We will deal with it," he said firmly.

She kept her mouth shut.

CHAPTER 11

1941—Chicago

December 7th, a chilly Chicago Sunday, changed everything. Lena and Karl had put Max down for a nap. Lena decided to make a batch of latkes for Hanukkah, which would start in a week's time. She was looking forward to the fact that Max might actually understand some of what the holiday was about this year.

Karl was working from home. He was not supposed to bring home any materials from the office, but he never discussed them with Lena, and she didn't ask. Otherwise, Lena and Max might never have seen him—he was so absorbed in his research. In July, a report from the British indicated that a nuclear weapon was a distinct possibility, and the Brits were going ahead with development.

Their enthusiasm spurred the Americans to re-analyze their findings. In November, Compton's committee concluded that a critical mass of between two and one hundred kilograms of uranium-235 would produce a powerful fission bomb, and that for fifty to one hundred million dollars it could be built.

Lena, who was chopping onions and enjoying their aroma, turned on the radio. The Bears football game was on. The broadcast was interrupted around 1:30 PM with the news that the Japanese were bombing the Pacific fleet in Pearl Harbor, Hawaii. Lena clapped a hand over her mouth. Karl stopped working and they remained glued to the radio for the rest of the day. Nearly twenty American ships, including eight enormous battleships, and almost two hundred airplanes were destroyed. Over two thousand Americans soldiers and sailors died; another thousand were wounded.

A day later, while officials were still sorting out

the damage, FDR went to Congress and delivered a short speech calling December 7th "a date which will live in infamy." Barely an hour later, Congress declared war on Japan. Three days after that the country was at war with Germany.

Lena descended into an unremitting state of anxiety. America was on the right side, but nothing was certain. She knew that events could—and did—change in an instant. The anti-Semitic laws in Europe, her flight from Germany, the loss of Josef, her parents' silence, *Kristallnacht*. She felt powerless, like a tennis ball buffeted back and forth across the net, with no will of its own. The security she'd been able to create with Karl and Max rested on the precarious feathers of history. The slightest change could scatter everything to oblivion.

Ironically, her mood was at odds with the rest of the country. Bravado and cheerfulness prevailed, as though Americans were relieved, excited, even cocky about going to war. "Slap the Japs" could be heard in bars, people talked about "Jap hunting" licenses, and reprisals against Japanese-Americans began.

Japanese restaurants closed, their shop windows smashed. Americans boycotted everything

Japanese, and there was much cheering and jeering from Chinatown, Japan's sworn enemy. Lena couldn't help comparing what was happening to what she'd gone through in Germany, although it wasn't nearly as harsh. She was frightened at the prospect of war, but she couldn't make herself hate the Japanese people.

Still, as the country geared up, she went through her days silent and brooding, waiting for something else to happen. Something bad was coming. She couldn't sleep, couldn't eat, couldn't sit still. Even Max picked up on her tension and grew cranky.

* * *

It happened a week later. A layer of sleet glazed everything with a coating of ice. By evening it was covered by two inches of snow. The roads were covered with a deceptive white shroud. Karl would be walking home from the University, but he had no boots or scarf; the morning had been unusually sunny and mild for December. He was rarely home before midnight since Pearl Harbor anyway, so Lena didn't wait up.

She woke a few hours later and checked the

time. It was one in the morning, but Karl wasn't in bed beside her. He hadn't called either, which he usually did if he was going to be very late or decided to spend the night at the office. She peered out the window. More snow. He must be staying overnight at the department, she told herself. No one would be foolish enough to go out in this storm. She went back to bed.

She was startled awake by the insistent ringing of the doorbell. She looked at the clock. Three AM. Did Karl forget his key? He never had before. She wrapped her robe tightly around her, went to the door, and squinted through the peephole.

Two police officers stood outside, stamping their feet in the snow. Her pulse thundered in her ears, coursing through her hands, chest, and head. It was hard to breathe. What did they want? Were they coming for her? Or Karl? Why?

For an instant she was back in Nazi Germany. But this was America. Karl had suggested she keep a gun in the house. She'd refused, telling him they were safe here. That even the thought of a weapon was ridiculous. Now, she wasn't so sure.

She cracked open the door, her hands trembling. "Yes?" Her voice was a hoarse whisper.

"Are you Mrs. Stern?"

She swallowed and nodded.

"I'm Officer O'Grady. And this is my partner, Officer Maywood. May we come in?"

"What do you want?"

"We need to talk to you about your husband."

Lena's stomach clenched, and she sagged against the door. Suddenly all she wanted to do was hurry back to bed and pull the covers over her head.

"Please, ma'am. Could you open the door?" O'Grady hesitated, as if he knew she was afraid. "We mean you no harm."

She sized up the officers. Bundled up in overcoats, boots, and gloves, they didn't appear to be carrying weapons. In fact the one called O'Grady took off his cap. Snowflakes melted on its brim. She opened the door wider.

"Thank you ma'am." They came in and stood just inside the doorway. She closed it and planted herself in front of it.

"I'm afraid we have some bad news, Mrs. Stern."

A steel band wrapped itself around her head.

"Your husband is Karl Stern?"

She nodded.

O'Grady took a breath. It sounded like a sigh.

"We responded to a call of an accident in the snow. It was a hit and run. On 57th Street."

The steel band tightened. Lena felt rooted to the floor.

"About an hour ago your husband was walking east on 57th Street. We believe he was coming from the University. That—"

She cut them off. "What happened?"

O'Grady looked down, away, then met her gaze. "Your husband was hit by an automobile. The driver must have lost control on the ice. The car hit him broadside. I'm sorry, Mrs. Stern, he didn't make it. He's dead."

CHAPTER 12

January, 1942—Chicago

*H*ashem was punishing Lena. He must be. At some point God must have ordained that she would never be happy for long. Was it because of the kisses she and Josef stole behind the trees in the Tiergarten? Because she had survived and her parents apparently had not? Perhaps it was because she hadn't put enough faith in Him over the years. She had worked to create her own life, her own happiness. It was clear now that God did not approve.

She endured the funeral, thick clouds of grief fogging her mind. The interment, too. Ursula organized the *shivah*, and for seven days people filed in and out. Compton came several times, sat with her, and held her hand. She didn't remember his words; all she recalled was that his glasses picked up the reflection of the lamp across the room. The German students from the department, scientists themselves now, came. So did her friend, Bonnie, from the Math Department, and people she didn't know who said they knew Karl.

Max couldn't understand where Papa had gone. He must be hiding, he said, and hunted for him under the beds, in the closets, behind doors. He kept asking her when Papa would be back. At one point he asked,

"Papa fight war?"

Lena's jaw dropped. Max wasn't even three years old. How was he able to make a connection between the war and his father's disappearance? She tried to explain.

"No, *liebchen*. Papa has gone to heaven."

"When come back?"

The lump in her throat was so thick she thought it might choke her. "He's not."

She gathered Max in her arms and hugged him tight. At the same time, she couldn't help thinking how her life had been marked by momentous yet horrific events. Max was born a few days after war was declared. Now Karl had been killed a few days after Pearl Harbor. What was next?

Officers O'Grady and Maywood were replaced by a detective accompanied by a man who introduced himself as FBI Special Agent Lanier. Lena stiffened. Probably in his forties, he was short but muscular with wispy blond hair.

"FBI? Why are you here?"

He smiled. "It's just a formality. We keep tabs on everyone at the Lab."

"Why?" Lena asked.

"There are some very special people working there," he said amiably.

Lena didn't respond.

The detective told Lena they'd canvassed the neighborhood, but no one recalled a car sliding across 57th Street at three in the morning. Everyone had been tucked up in bed. But they would keep looking, he promised. She saw in his eyes he was lying.

* * *

The end of the year holidays were desolate. Lena

remembered how she and Karl would spend New Year's Eve with the other physicists in the department. They would go up to the Loop to hear jazz or Swing music and dance until midnight. Not this year. Ursula brought over chicken and red cabbage, but it went untouched.

Two weeks later Ursula rang the doorbell. It was well past noon, but Lena hadn't bothered to dress herself or Max. In her usual efficient way, Ursula made them bathe and put on clothes. Then she cleaned the house and made tea.

When they were seated at the kitchen table, Ursula stirred sugar into her tea. "So my dear, what are your plans?"

Lena looked up, trying to blink away the fog. She shrugged.

Ursula nodded. "Yes. You have been through hell. Still, it is time to think about moving forward."

Lena groped for a reply, but it seemed as if Ursula was speaking a foreign language. She had no idea what to say.

Ursula went on. "It has been over thirty days since Karl passed. I know you're still grieving, but it is time to start picking up your life."

Lena kept her mouth shut.

"What is your money situation?"

"We are scraping by."

"So," Ursula said in a matter-of-fact tone, "you will need to go back to work."

"How can I? What about Max?"

"We will find someone to look after him. Perhaps the lady who lives upstairs. The one whose grandchildren come every week?"

Mrs. McNulty, a blowsy woman with fly-away white hair, lived upstairs. She never forgot to wink at Max whenever she saw him, and she always asked Lena how he was. In fact, Lena remembered her concerned expression among the sea of faces at the *shivah*. She'd brought down a bowl of fruit, Lena recalled. Apples, Max's favorite.

"But where? How can I make enough to support us both? And pay Mrs. McNulty?"

Ursula stared at Lena for a few seconds in silence then pursed her lips. "Surely, you remember."

"Remember what?"

"Professor Compton. He sat beside you for a long while one night at the *shivah*. He said your old job was waiting for you if you wanted it."

Lena shook her head. She had no memory of the conversation.

"I was right beside you, rubbing your back. He even said he understood you could not work late because of Max. He said you and he could work something out. They replaced you with another secretary, of course, but he said he could use a second as well."

Lena's eyes widened.

"It's time," Ursula said.

CHAPTER 13

January, 1942—Chicago

And so Lena went back to her job at the Physics department. It had never been a quiet place, but it was positively bustling now, a frantic urgency sweeping the air. Ever since America had entered the war, each day felt like a race against the clock.

Compton was at the helm, spearheading experiments in fission from coast to coast. Each project, from Enrico Fermi's at Columbia University in New York, to J. Robert Oppenheimer's at Berkeley, would hopefully forge a path to a nuclear device. Lena and Sonia, the other secretary, kept busy sending frequent letters, sometimes telegrams, to the scientists; typing conclusions and analyses by other physicists; even corresponding with government officials. Lena was thrilled to be interacting, albeit indirectly, with the most famous scientists in the country. Bit by bit, she started to emerge from her shell of grief.

Shortly after she returned, Compton decided to combine some of the research programs into one location. He appointed Leo Szilard head of materials acquisition and convinced Szilard, Fermi, and others to move to Chicago. He snagged some unused space beneath a racquetball court under the west grandstand of Stagg Field and created what became known as the Metallurgical Lab. It was here that the department would build the machinery to conduct experiments with graphite and uranium that, when bombarded with neutrons, would, hopefully, produce a chain reaction.

At home life seemed to fall into place as well. Max enjoyed his days with Mrs. McNulty, whom he called Mrs. M.

"All he wants to eat are apples," Mrs. M said.

"That's not necessarily bad," Lena said.

Mrs. McNulty smiled. "And when he's not munching on the fruit, he plays with Lincoln Logs. I think he's going to be an engineer when he grows up. Or a scientist."

"Like his father," Lena said softly.

She tried to spend as much time as she could with Max after work and begged Mrs. McNulty to let him nap long hours so she could keep him up at night. He was chattering non-stop now, and Lena loved teaching him new words and ideas. But even with a three-hour nap, his little head drooped by nine in the evening, so she would sing him some of the German lullabies her mother sang to her, tuck him in bed, then fall asleep herself.

Between food, rent, and Mrs. McNulty, Lena was barely making it financially. Every week she plunged deeper in debt. The kindly grocer extended endless lines of credit, Mrs. McNulty, too. Still, Lena worried she could never repay what she owed. She feared it was just a matter of time until it all unraveled.

CHAPTER 14

———

April, 1942—Chicago

Lena picked up the phone at work one rainy morning just before lunch. Compton had been expecting a call from Fermi who was in the midst of moving to Chicago. When he called, she was to find Compton immediately. So she was expecting a male voice on the other end of the line. Instead she heard a sobbing woman, whose obvious anguish made her words incomprehensible.

"Hello? Who is this?"

More crying, followed by a sharp intake of breath.

"Please, who is there?"

"Mi-Mrs., Stern," She stammered. "It's—it's Mabel McNulty."

It took Lena a moment to register the caller. They always addressed each other as Mrs. Stern or Mrs. M. But when she realize who it was, a bolt of fear streaked up her spine. "What's the matter? Is Max all right?"

"The—the police are here."

Panic surged through Lena. She began to shiver uncontrollably. "The police? What happened?"

"Mrs. Stern, I can't believe it." Her voice cracked. "I don't know—I just don't know how it happened."

"Mrs. McNulty," Lena was shouting now, so loud that Sonia looked up from her desk in alarm. "Where is Max?"

A fresh stream of crying filled her ears. Lena jumped up. With her free hand she grabbed her purse. A swish came over the telephone line, and a deep male voice said,

"Mrs. Stern? This is Officer Delgado. Chicago Police Department."

Lena's stomach clenched, and a wave of nausea worked its way up to her throat.

"Your boy, Max—has been kidnapped. We're sending a squad car to pick you up."

* * *

Mrs. McNulty and Max were on their way back from the Museum of Science and Industry where Max loved to wander through the Coal Mine exhibit, Mrs. M said. She had brought the stroller in case he was tired, but Max wanted to walk by himself. She always held his hand when they walked outside, but this morning Mrs. M was juggling the stroller and an umbrella as well as Max. They had just reached the bend in the road that turned into 57th Street when someone raced up behind Mrs. M, shoved her, and snatched Max.

The movement was so sudden and aggressive that Mrs. M fell to the ground. She screamed and so did Max, but just then a car pulled up behind them and slowed. The man who had Max opened the back door and threw himself and the boy into the back. The car sped off.

Everything happened so fast that Mrs. M didn't have time to catch the license plate. Not that it would help. It would take hours, if not days, to find the DMV record of the auto. Mrs. M raced home to call the police.

Lena didn't remember the ride in the squad car, but twenty minutes later, she was talking to two policemen in her living room. Officers were combing the area, they said; they were marshalling all their resources to find Max.

But they were at a disadvantage. They didn't know the make of the car—all Mrs. M could recall was a dark sedan. They didn't have a license plate either, or a solid description of the kidnapper. Still, they were canvassing neighbors, and cruisers were parked at 57th Street to stop and question motorists. They sent cops to the Museum to interview the guards and staff. A photo of Max had been circulated and was being posted. No one wanted another Leopold and Loeb.

Lena listened as the officers explained, but their voices seemed to be muffled by a thick hazy blanket. She felt distanced from the conversation, as though she didn't quite understand what they were saying. In a corner of her brain she knew she was in shock, but she had no idea how to deal with it. She sat on her sofa, hands folded politely in her lap, as if she were listening to a piano concerto.

FBI Agent Lanier, the same agent who'd come when Karl died, showed up thirty minutes later. Mrs. M went through her story again, shooting apologetic glances at Lena.

When Mrs. M finished, Lanier told Lena to stay at home and near the phone. "The chances are good whoever has Max will make a ransom call before long."

"But I can't pay. I have no money." It was the first thing she'd said since Lanier arrived.

"They don't know that. They probably think Mrs. McNulty is a nanny or governess, and you live in one of those big homes on Hyde Park Avenue. The two of them were perfect marks."

Lena made a sound that wasn't quite a sob. "I'm a secretary at the University. It's all I can do to put food on the table."

"You're working at Met Lab again, right?"

"Yes. The Physics Department."

Lanier nodded, as if he was confirming what he already knew, and changed the subject. He didn't press her about the work going on there, but Lena couldn't tell him if he did. She'd signed a strict confidentiality agreement when she went back.

She could speak of it to no one, including the authorities.

Time seemed to stop that afternoon. After the police officers left, it was quiet except for the plunk of raindrops against the windows. Lena didn't move from her spot on the sofa. Agent Lanier stayed but didn't talk much. Around five he said he was going back to the office, but another detective would arrive. As he opened the door to leave, he gave her explicit instructions.

"When you get the call, call me immediately. They'll tell you not to, but you must. We'll be working in the background to get your boy back." He paused. "Mrs. Stern, there are good reasons to think he will be returned safely. More than one person was involved. Which means it was a conspiracy. They took him for a reason. Probably money. If it had been just one man, we'd be looking at a more ominous situation. Don't lose faith."

He left and closed the door softly. Faith? Lena had no faith. Watching raindrops dribble sideways across a window, she knew, again, that she must have done something very wicked to warrant the punishments that had befallen her. Why had God chosen her?

Slowly she rose from the sofa and trudged into the kitchen. She took a tall glass from the cabinet and filled it with water. She drank about half, then examined the glass. She turned around and hurled the glass across the room. It smashed against the opposite wall and exploded, flinging shards of glass and water across the floor. The sound of shattering glass was oddly comforting.

CHAPTER 15

———

The telephone call came after Lanier left but before the police detective arrived. Lena had just finished cleaning up the broken glass, and the ring startled her. She raced to the phone, then hesitated. Why now? Who knew she would be alone at this precise moment?

"I assume the detective has left." It was a gruff male voice, but it was muffled as if he was speaking through a towel or blanket.

"Who is this?"

"Someone you want to talk to. Is the baby sitter gone?"

———

Mrs. M, still hysterical, had gone up to her apartment to try and calm down.

Someone had been watching her apartment. Lena started to tremble. "I—I'm alone." She stammered.

"Good. We have Max. He's fine. And we want to bring him back."

"Thank god. Please bring him right away."

"We will. But we want something in return."

Her stomach twisted. She bit her lip. "I have no money."

There was a laugh on the other end of the line. A laugh! "We know. In fact, we will help you change that."

"What—what are you saying?"

"We want to reimburse you for your pain and suffering. God knows you've had your share."

"How do you know that? Who are you? I want my son!"

"You will get him. But you must agree to our proposition."

"What proposition?"

"A man will be coming to your home in a few minutes. He will be wearing a policeman's uniform. But he is not an officer. You will let him in. Do you understand?"

"Yes, but—"

"Once you have agreed to the proposition, Max will be returned."

"Tonight? You'll bring him back tonight?"

"Yes. We have not harmed him. And we don't want to."

"What if I cannot accept the proposition? What if I refuse?"

"That would not be a good idea, Lena. For you or Max."

* * *

The man to whom Lena opened the door was unremarkable in every way. Average height, average weight, average thinning brown hair. Horn-rimmed glasses. His only distinguishing feature was a pair of oversized ears. Dressed in a cop's uniform, he had a badge pinned to his chest. If she'd been asked to describe him later, she wouldn't have been able to provide much.

He deposited himself on the sofa where she'd been sitting just a few minutes earlier. She picked up the baby blanket she'd been holding to remind her of Max's smell, and sat in the chair.

"Is Max all right? What have you done with him?"

He cleared his throat. "He is fine. But I only have a few minutes, Frau Stern, so here's what we want." He paused. "Information." He spoke with an unmistakable accent. It was German. From the South. Probably Bavaria. Reinhard, Ursula's husband, had a similar accent, and he was from Regensburg.

She folded her arms. "What information?" she said in German.

His eyes narrowed for a quick moment, and she saw in his expression that under the right circumstances he was probably capable of enormous cruelty. Despite the heat in the apartment, she shivered again. He must have realized his effect on her, because he unexpectedly bared his teeth in what she supposed was a smile.

"Information you come by on a daily basis." He answered in English.

She didn't reply at first. She was trying to process why he hadn't answered in German. Then she cast the thought aside. If that's what he wanted to do, what choice did she have? She wanted her son. "So you want me to spy at my job," she said in English.

The smile that wasn't really a smile widened. "They said you were a quick study."

"Who are you working for?" She asked, although she really didn't need to. It was clear. "You want me to spy for the Nazis?"

He didn't confirm it but didn't disagree.

"Why would I ever do that? After what you—they did to me? To my family? To my life? I'd rather die than help those—you monsters."

He nodded, as if he wasn't surprised at her reaction. "I understand. But there is really only one point to consider. If you do not comply, you will never see your son again."

She stared at the man, then let her head sink into her hands. The tears that refused to come earlier now welled. Her life consisted of a series of events she could not control. Now there was one more.

The fake cop cleared his throat. "Frau Stern, we do not have much time. Another police officer will arrive soon."

Once more she was trapped. She had to play along. She breathed in the scent of the blanket.

Without Max, life was not worth living. She hoped God would forgive her. Then she scoffed at the thought. There was no God. At least for her. That was abundantly clear. She looked over, blinking through her tears.

"What is it you want me to do?"

"We want you to bring us whatever you come across in your daily work. Letters, files, theoretical analyses, observations. Photos of the Lab, if you can. It is clear America is committed to building an atomic weapon, and we know there are several paths to that end. We know Chicago is working on one option. We need to know what your scientists know. As soon as they know it. You will provide it."

"But what happens if they find out?" She repeated. "Will you help me escape? Find someplace for Max and me to disappear to?"

The man cleared his throat. "We understand this will not be easy. Or risk free. It is quite possible someone at some point will suspect what you are doing."

The answer was no, she thought. They would do nothing if she was unmasked. She was on her own.

"That is why we are willing to compensate you.

Generously," he went on. "We will pay you two hundred dollars a month."

Her mouth opened. It was a fortune. Her money problems would disappear. "We know you have had financial problems since the untimely death of your husband."

Untimely? What did that mean, "untimely"? She peered at him, but his expression remained flat. Then he cocked his head.

"A word of warning, Lena. Do not think you can get away from us. We are watching you. We know every step that you take. Once you start down this road, there is no going back."

Lena hated this man and his words. But she couldn't go to the authorities. She was a German herself. A refugee. And although she was now a U.S. citizen, every German was suspect these days. They might even decide she was already spying. Then what would happen to her and Max? She couldn't risk it. She was trapped.

The man looked at his watch. "I must leave." He cleared his throat. "But there is one other matter. You will need to learn tradecraft."

"What does that mean, tradecraft?"

"There are many ways to retrieve and exchange

information. You will learn the basic techniques. I will teach you."

"You're going to teach me how to be a spy!"

"I wouldn't call it that."

"What would you call it?" She knew she sounded irritated. She wanted him to get that.

"Methods to manage your risk. And ours." He hesitated. "So. What is your answer?"

She stared and took a deep breath, hoping it would make him uncomfortable. "You give me no choice."

The man pulled out an envelope from his jacket pocket. He opened it and counted out ten twenty dollar bills which he laid on the coffee table.

Her mouth fell open again.

"You need not see me out. We start training tomorrow. You will find a note in your mailbox with the meeting time and location."

Lena picked up the money. "Since we are to be working together, what is your name?"

"You may call me Hans."

She nodded. "What about Max, Hans? "

He rose from the sofa. "Your son will be dropped off shortly."

The promise was kept. Ten minutes later, the

buzzer rang. Lena raced down the steps. As she opened the front door, a car pulled away, leaving Max standing on the curb. He held a balloon in one hand, and a small cherry lollypop in the other. His lips were stained red, as if he'd been sucking on it for hours.

"Hello, Mama," He grinned.

She closed her arms around him.

CHAPTER 16

———

"Americans are suspicious of everything," Hans told Lena a week later. "But they must not be suspicious of you."

They were walking down State Street in the Loop on a crisp Saturday morning in April. It was still early, and the sun slanted through the buildings and bounced off shop windows in a cheerful display of light. "You must always be aware of your surroundings, the environment, and the people. Be alert for someone or something that could compromise your security. It might be quite small and inconsequential, and it will probably be the one thing that doesn't belong." He stopped.

"For example, what color was the dress of the woman who just passed us?"

Hans had a fast stride, and Lena was concentrating on keeping pace with him. She had no idea about the dress. "I don't know," she said.

"Turn around."

She did. The dress was powder blue. She turned back.

"What about her shoes?"

Lena's spirits sank. It was one thing to make sure she didn't bump into people as they hurried down the street. It was quite another to remember what shoes they were wearing.

"They were black," he said. "Was she wearing perfume?"

Lena shrugged.

As if reading her mind, he went on. "She was. But do not worry. It will come. The point is, you must not do anything to raise an alarm... to make people think their security is at stake. But *your* security is critical. If it seems too much of a risk, if you think someone is tailing you, abort the mission. Figure out how to accomplish it a different way."

Hans had been training Lena for five days.

Despite the fact it was hard to leave Max, she had worked with Hans every evening after work and now today. He had divided her education into subjects. Today was surveillance. He was teaching her how to tell if she was being followed, and if so, how to lose the tail. He was also showing her how to tail someone else, although he admitted she likely wouldn't have much use for it. Her primary activity was simply to supply information about the research and development going on at Met Lab. Still, he said, she should be familiar with basic techniques.

They had already discussed communication. She would buy a flowerpot for her windowsill, he said, and move it from one side to the other to signal a meet or indicate something was in the dead drop. He also taught her to watch for signals from him. How to follow chalk marks, bottle caps, orange peels, or tacks affixed to telephone poles. He pointed out two dead drops both within a block of her apartment, where she would leave rolls of film and documents. She was surprised she'd never noticed them before; then again, that was the point. He taught her how to spot a classified ad in the newspaper that was really a coded message and how to decrypt it. Her brain was swimming.

"And those are just the simple methods," he'd reminded her.

The next area they needed to discuss, he said, as they continued down State, were tools. "You will clearly need a camera so you can take pictures of the set up as well as documents."

Lena frowned. "But how—"

He cut her off. "Of course we would prefer the actual documents, but we know in your case that will not be possible. Photos will suffice. You will leave a roll of film in the dead drop every time you have something."

"What if I'm not able to take photos?"

"You will find a way. Work late. Come in early."

"Everyone already does."

"Then go in earlier. Stay later. Go in on a weekend."

"And how am I supposed to get the film out of the office?"

He waved a hand. "Your purse. A briefcase. You will figure it out."

"I don't carry a briefcase. It would look pretentious if I began."

"Improvise. A grocery bag. Your coat pockets. Here." He stopped walking, pulled out his wallet, and peeled off a twenty. "Go into Marshall Fields and buy a new bag. A big one."

Lena didn't miss a beat. "And the camera?"

He laughed. "You learn quickly. We will supply it. Go into the store. I will wait."

They were standing under the clock at State and Randolph. She headed towards the store entrance. Then she turned around and came back. "What about a gun?"

"A gun? For you?"

She nodded.

"No gun."

She spun around and went into Fields.

CHAPTER 17

———

Much to Lena's chagrin, Agent Lanier came around twice after the incident. He claimed he couldn't figure out who had taken and then returned Max with no questions asked.

Hans had told Lena what to say. "I have no idea," she recited. "What do you think?"

"Like I said, I don't know. I really thought it was a ransom case."

"Agent Lanier," she smiled. "Perhaps you did a better job than you thought. Perhaps the people who took him knew they couldn't get away with it." She barreled on. "I'm just grateful to have him back. I never want to go through that again.

———

Especially so soon after my husband's death." She swallowed and bit her lip, as if she was trying to suppress tears.

He scratched his cheek. "Yeah, that is a factor. I can't help but wonder whether the two incidents are related."

Lena went pale.

"Oh come on, Mrs. Stern. Surely the same thought has crossed your mind."

She didn't answer for a moment. "Of course it has. But how? For what purpose?"

He cocked his head. "I was hoping you could tell me."

"You must remember I lost my parents. My homeland. My husband. And then I almost lost my son." She shook her head. "Agent Lanier, I cannot survive another loss."

After a long moment, he nodded. "I understand. I'll leave you in peace. But, I want to—"

"Yes?"

"I think we know each other well enough to use first names, don't you? I'm Ted. But everyone calls me Terry."

Lena smiled. "Lena."

"Here's my card. If you ever need anything, feel free to call."

* * *

Hans fabricated a story to tell the people at Met Lab about Max. Lena was to say he had not been kidnapped after all. He had simply wandered off from Mrs. M and got lost. He'd been found by a Good Samaritan and returned a few hours later. Everyone seemed to accept it, which made Lena feel guilty. Compton had gone out of his way to rehire her after Karl died. Adjusted her schedule so she could be with Max. Even kept on Sonia, the other secretary, to share the load. And the way she repaid him? Lies and duplicity.

Indeed, her stomach pitched every time she thought about what she was doing. But when the money arrived promptly each week in fifty dollar increments, it made a difference. She began to pay off the grocers' bill. For the first time since Karl died, she could afford the rent, and she even had a little extra to lavish on Max. She came to depend on the money and started to see her job through a different lens. Everything she handled or saw could be measured by whether she could snap photos of it, and how much it paid.

It wasn't difficult to monitor the goings-on at the Lab. Major events seemed to occur every day. Fermi was now working in Chicago along with Glenn Seaborg and Leo Szilard, and someone named Bush was the liaison between Compton and the President.

The first document she photographed was a letter from Bush to Compton about the Army Corps of Engineers, who had been tasked with building whatever weapon was created. Several officers were named as key contacts, and she knew Hans and his people would want to know who they were. Hans had given her a tiny camera called a Minox. About the size and shape of a small comb, it fit easily in her bag or pocket and was perfect for photographing documents. It had been designed by a German, he said.

A few days later, on a rain-soaked afternoon that made Lena glad she was inside, she told Sonia that she would stay until it stopped. She'd forgotten to bring her umbrella. "You know how unpredictable Chicago weather is."

"Why don't you take mine?" Sonia said. "My sister is coming to pick me up. I'll share hers."

Lena's stomach clenched, and her pulse sped up. "Oh no. I have work to do, anyway."

Sonia glanced over and smiled. "Well then, take it when you leave. I know you'll bring it back."

Lena bit her lip. "Thank you," she managed. She hoped she sounded casual, but her insides were churning. Had she sounded ungrateful? Too dismissive? Would Sonia suspect something? Some spy, she thought. Her first assignment and she was already worried about exposure. Maybe she should just go to Compton and confess. How could she live with this kind of stress every time she chatted with a colleague? If she did confess, though, what would Hans and his people do to Max? As long as they were around, her son would never be free from their clutches, whoever "they" were. And she was sure "they" were Nazis. She kept her mouth shut.

It wasn't until nine that evening that she was finally alone in the office. Everything was quiet, except for the buzz of the fluorescent lights and the trickle of rain on the windows. She waited another minute, then went to the filing cabinets, which stood behind her and Sonia's desk. They were locked, but she and Sonia had keys. She unlocked the nearest cabinet and pulled out the top drawer. The files were arranged chronologically, and the letter Bush had written to Compton was in front. She laid the paper on top of the cabinet, then thought better of it, and brought it back to her desk.

Slipping the Minox out of her bag, she paused, listening for any change in the ambient sound. Nothing. But she could smell the fear on herself, and her hands shook so much she had to take half a dozen photos of the letter. When she was finished, she dropped the camera into her bag, hurriedly put the letter back, and relocked the cabinet. She grabbed her bag and rushed out.

She was almost home, making record time despite the rain, when she realized she'd left Sonia's umbrella at the office. An icicle of fear slid around her stomach. What should she do? She couldn't lie and say the rain had stopped; it was still coming down at a steady rate. But if she didn't bring it in tomorrow, Sonia might suspect something. Better to be safe. She trudged back to the department to fetch the umbrella, then retraced her way home.

Inside the front hall she shook out the umbrella and practically ran up the stairs to her apartment. Max was fast asleep, and Mrs. M was snoring in the living room. Lena tiptoed further into her son's room and kissed him on the forehead. It took thirty minutes before her breathing returned to normal.

CHAPTER 18

_____

After a month it was easier. There were even times when Lena felt justified in her behavior. She had found a way to strike back at the events that had defined her life. She was no longer at the whim of fate. She was taking action. In control. She enjoyed the money, too. In fact, taking money from the Nazis gave her a perverse sense of satisfaction. She bought new clothes for herself and Max, and put a new sofa and easy chair for the living room on layaway.

One morning she wore a new navy blue dress with white polka dots and a huge bow to work. When Sonia caught sight of her, she whistled.

"Well hi-de-ho! Aren't you the pretty picture!" She cocked her head. "You have a new boyfriend or something?"

Lena felt her cheeks get hot. "Of course not. It has only been six months since Karl died."

Sonia looked her over. "Well then, I guess I'd better ask Compton for the same raise you got," she said.

Lena made a mental note not to wear new clothes to the office again. And although part of her was secretly proud of her newfound ability to provide for herself and Max, part of her, too, was ashamed at the source of the money.

The worst times were when she ran into Compton. Her pulse would speed up, her cheeks grew hot. She was sure he could see straight through her, and was waiting to confront her. She imagined what Hester Prynne must have felt like wearing that scarlet letter across her chest. On those days she'd rush home from work, clasp Max in her arms, and cry.

* * *

Hans didn't signal for a meeting until June. She was on her way to work, the morning bright and full of the promise of summer. June usually reminded Lena of her wedding day, but today, tears didn't spring to her eyes. Indeed, this was new, this sense of satisfaction. Was this what it was like to feel like she belonged? To own a tiny piece of the American dream? Despite the war, despite what was happening in Europe, despite everything, she had resources. Perhaps she could look the other way, pretend the nefarious work she was doing didn't exist.

She was so wrapped up in this new thought, turning it this way and that in her mind, that she almost missed the orange peel on the corner of 57th and Kimbark. As soon as she spotted it, she squeezed her eyes shut. She couldn't pretend. As much as she wanted to imagine, this wasn't make-believe.

At lunch she told Sonia she was going out for a walk and headed towards the Museum of Science and Industry. She wandered around the main floor, admiring the high ceilings and massive columns of the former Palace of Fine Arts. Julius Rosenwald, the chairman of Sears, Roebuck and Company, got the idea for the museum after visiting a similar place in Munich thirty years earlier with his son. The Rosenwalds held a special place in Lena's heart. Rosenwald's son, William, organized an effort in the mid-1930s to help Jews in Nazi Germany emigrate to the US. Some people *did* do the right thing, she mused. Of course, they had the money and means.

She was thinking about how life could surprise you with its decency when Hans appeared at her side. He took her arm, as if they were lovers about to steal a precious hour together. They strolled to an area where workmen were building a miniature train and village that would fill an entire wing. The exhibit was to open at Christmas.

"You are well, Lena?" Hans asked.

"Very. And you?" She answered cautiously.

"I am fine." A small smile crossed his face. "So. We have a new priority for you."

She raised her eyebrows.

"We know that American scientists are trying to build chain-reacting 'Piles' to produce plutonium, and then extract it from the irradiated uranium so they can build an atomic bomb. We want you to focus on the Pile and the tests that are planned in it."

She tried to hide her surprise. "How do you know this?"

"Come, Lena. You must realize you are not our only asset." He laughed. "Although you are certainly the most attractive."

Lena blew out a breath.

"We know that a group headed by Compton's chief engineer, Thomas Moore, began designing the Pile under the west stands of Stagg Field."

"Tell me, Hans, who is 'we'? Haven't I proven myself enough to tell me about the others in your group?"

Hans raised a finger to his lips. "We need the plans for the Pile."

She hesitated. Then, "I know I have made a pact with the devil, but I need more specifics. It will help me tailor what I give you."

"Lena, let's keep to the subject at hand. We need to find out how they are building the Pile."

"But that is impossible. I am not allowed anywhere near it."

"There must be a blueprint."

"If there is, neither Sonia nor I have high enough clearances to see it."

"Then you'll have to think of a way to get the information."

"How? I can't break in. There are guards there all night."

Hans clasped his free hand over hers. "You're a resourceful woman. You will find a way."

CHAPTER 19

———

Lena's mood deteriorated after the meet with Hans. She was dirty, scheming, worse than a tease. In fact, she was nothing more than a whore for the Nazis—supplying information rather than sex. But this was her lot. She had agreed to it. And so over the next few days she studied the scientists at the Met Lab, particularly the younger ones, wondering who would become her unwitting accomplice.

She finally settled on Irving Mandell, a shy, self-effacing young man from the South Side who had stayed at the university after earning his Ph.D. He worked on the Pile, and she knew he held the highest clearance possible. He was skinny and tall

———

with curly black hair that resembled a messy bird's nest and an acne-scarred face. His eyes were large and soulful, but he wore a perpetually timid expression.

She made sure she was at her desk when he came and went each day and started with cheery "good mornings" and "good nights." That led to brief conversations and lots of smiles on her part. At one point, two weeks later, after one conversation, she ran to the ladies room, afraid she was going to vomit. She didn't recognize herself. What had she become?

Sonia followed her in with a worried frown. "You're as white as Casper's ghost. What's wrong?"

Lena shook her head.

Sonia's eyes narrowed. That was not a good sign. Lena would have to be more careful.

Two weeks after that, it paid off. She and Irving had shared coffee on one occasion, lunch on another, and this evening they'd met for a beer at the restaurant she and Karl used to frequent. Lena always kept the conversation focused on physics and work. "I've always wanted to understand better," She said. "But I never had the chance to study. You know, coming from Germany when I did..." She let her voice trail off.

Irving nodded earnestly. Although he wasn't aware of it, he had played his part perfectly. He was by turns the eager scholar, the wise teacher, the ardent suitor. Lena was sure no woman had ever paid him this much attention, and she felt a stab of guilt every time she flashed him a smile or brushed his hand with her fingers, as she did now.

He launched into an explanation of how plutonium could theoretically be separated from irradiated uranium.

"Is that what you're doing in the Pile?"

"That's part of it. You see if we can successfully do that, we can then manufacture as much as we need. And then..." He frowned. "You know, I'm not supposed to talk about it with anyone. Including co-workers."

She looked over. "Of course, you're not. I'm sorry. I don't mean to—" She let her voice trail off.

"What?" He asked.

She lifted a shoulder, then shook her head. "Nothing."

His expression softened. "What is it, Lena?"

"I—I would love to see the Pile. Is it safe to go in?"

"Oh yes."

"No chance of people getting irradiated, is there?"

"None whatsoever." He laughed. "Tell me, Lena, why is the Pile so important?"

She looked down. "It's—it's just that we—you and I and all the others—will be a part of history. What you are doing will change the world forever."

He folded his arms.

"I— guess I just wanted to share a tiny little part of it. I long to see it. Even just for a few seconds." She flashed him a sad smile. "Still, I understand. You can not compromise security."

Irving let out a sigh. He looked left, then right, as if he thought someone might be watching. "I would love to show it to you," he said. "But I can't take the chance."

Lena nodded, as if resigned to his decision. "Let's talk about something else, shall we?" She glanced at her watch. "Oh, dear, it's after seven. I really must get home. Max and Mrs. M will wonder what has become of me."

Irving leaned over the table and kissed her

cheek. She brushed his cheek with her fingers. "You are the best thing that's ever happened to me," he said.

"You don't mind that I'm an old woman?" she teased. She was three years older.

"Are you kidding? The rest of the guys are jealous."

"You've told them about us?" She tried to make herself blush. "Oh no."

"Was I wrong?" A worried frown came over him.

She didn't reply for a moment. Then she smiled prettily. "I—I guess not."

They both rose from the table. He clasped her hand in his. "Come. I will walk you home."

"You do not have to."

"I know."

But outside the restaurant he turned west, not east, which was the way to Lena's apartment. She pulled on his arm. "We should be going the other way, Irving."

He took her hand again. "Where we're going you must never speak of. Ever. Do you understand?"

Her stomach flipped. "I understand," she whispered. "It never happened."

They walked the few blocks toward Stagg Field.

CHAPTER 20

———

They arrived at the stadium and walked around to the western corner. The evening was hot and humid; within minutes, sweat ringed Lena's neck. She wiped a handkerchief across her brow.

"Stay here," Irving said and ducked inside.

Lena gazed at the field's brick exterior, much of it covered by ivy. At each corner, a turret rose above the structure like a well-guarded castle. Windows above the first floor were shaded with awnings, while bars covered the windows at ground level. If she walked through the gate, she would eventually find herself in the middle of the field, the seats in the open like the bleachers at Wrigley.

The lack of protection made for icy football games, and she'd never attended one. She never understood why Americans thought a group of burly young men attacking each other and hurling them to the ground was sporting. It was barbaric, not at all like the civilized football—or soccer, as they called it in the US—she'd known in Europe.

Irving came back out, jogged across the street, and reached for her hand. "Come quickly." He sounded out of breath.

"Are you sure?"

He reached down and kissed her.

She returned it. "You will not get into trouble?"

"If I do," he smiled, "it will have been worth it."

They walked through the entrance, down a flight of stairs, and around a corner to a closed door. There was no one outside.

"Where's the guard?"

Irving raised his palm in a gesture that said to keep quiet and fished a key out of his pocket. Unlocking the door with one hand, he ushered her inside with the other.

Lena wasn't sure what she'd expected. From her

memos and letters, she knew the Pile contained 771,000 pounds of graphite, 80,590 pounds of uranium oxide and 12,400 pounds of uranium metal. It cost one million dollars to build. The Pile was described as a flattened ellipsoid, constructed on the lattice principle with graphite as a moderator and lumps of metal or oxide. They were the reacting units and were spaced through the graphite to form the lattice. Instruments situated at various points in the Pile or near it indicated the neutron intensity, and movable strips of absorbing material served as controls.

But that was the abstract definition. What she saw was a room, once a squash court, about twenty-five feet wide, its ceiling twenty feet high. At one end was a contraption that rose from floor to ceiling. Most of it was built out of bricks, with a brick wall in the center and what looked like terraced "piles" of bricks above it, each recessed more than the pile below. The ceiling above the Pile looked like it was made out of cushions, although Lena knew that wasn't the case. Behind the bricks, she knew from the letters she'd typed, were the tons of graphite, uranium oxide, and uranium metal.

Something resembling a long faucet protruded from the lowest pile, but again, Lena didn't know if water came out from it. A ladder leaned against the brick wall. To the right of the contraption was a set of stairs; on the other side, a thick curtain that might have been lead, which separated the Pile from the rest of the room. Adjacent to that was a series of cubicles about twelve feet high, each containing odd looking pieces of equipment, none of which she could identify.

Irving watched her gaze at the contraption with wide-eyed amazement. "So what do you think?"

"I—I don't know. I didn't know what to expect. It looks rather benign, actually. What do you call it? I mean, besides Pile Number 1? Is it going to be a bomb?"

"This is a nuclear reactor. It's very different from a bomb," he said with a touch of pride.

Lena furrowed her brow. "Then why build it? I mean, what does it do?"

"It would take a semester to explain it to you," he said, "but basically, a bomb requires a huge amount of fissionable material. So that's what we're trying to do—create a lot of fissionable material quickly."

"How do you do that?" she asked, becoming interested in spite of herself.

"That's what we're working out. We think it's by creating a chain reaction that will essentially 'cook' uranium and produce energy. While it's cooking, it forms plutonium, which we need for the bomb. Once it's cooled, we will try to separate the plutonium from the uranium. But the plutonium will be highly radioactive, so we have to build machines that can do all this by remote control."

"I had no idea."

Irving grinned. "Yes. But you see, there are other scientists around the country experimenting with other materials. It's almost a race to see which team produces results first. Of course, we think it will be us," Irving said with a hint of pride.

The sound of footsteps clattered outside the door to the reactor room. Irving's eyes went wide. "The guard is coming back. We have to get out." He grabbed her arm, and they sprinted to the stairs in the corner of the room. "Follow me."

* * *

Back home twenty minutes later, after a long goodnight kiss, Lena drew a sketch of the reactor.

She searched her memory to make sure she included all the details. She was nearly finished when the phone rang.

"Lena? It's Ursula."

"Hello. Are you all right? Is Reinhard?"

"We're fine, but I have some bad news."

Lena stiffened.

"We received a letter from friends back in Berlin. They said your parents were rounded up last year and resettled in the East."

Lena squeezed her eyes shut. "Where?"

"Who knows? The rumors are somewhere in Poland."

Lena nodded to herself. She'd gone to an occasional service at KAM Isaiah Israel where the rabbi told congregants what was really happening to the Jews in Europe.

Ursula paused. "I think you need to prepare yourself, *liebchen*. You have no doubt heard about the Nazis' Final Solution. There is little doubt about their future. I am so sorry."

Lena didn't reply for a moment. "I understand. Thank you, Ursula." She replaced the receiver quietly, as if any additional sound would break the telephone into pieces.

She went back to her sketch of the Pile. She wanted to tear it up, tell Hans she hadn't been able to complete the mission. Then she had a better idea. She stared at the drawing. She couldn't change it too much; Hans had told her she wasn't their only asset. Still, she was probably the only asset who'd actually been inside the Pile. She altered the sketch just enough, removing the faucets, the "booths" on the side of the Pile, and the cushiony material on the ceiling.

* * *

The next morning on her way to work, she sought out a crevice in a waist-high stone wall on Dorchester. It was the primary dead drop for her rolls of film, but the sketch, which she'd slipped into a white envelope, was too large for the space, and the envelope was clearly visible. Flicking an imaginary spot off her jacket, she glanced in both directions. No one was coming. She casually dropped the envelope back in her purse and returned home. She opened the curtains in the living room, raised the window, and moved the flowerpot filled with pansies to the other side of the sill.

Hans dropped by her apartment after work. The thick summer sun was still so punishing that even the shadows held no relief. Rings of sweat stained Lena's blouse under her armpits, but when Hans arrived, he was wearing a wool jacket. She was about to ask why he was torturing himself, but when she watched him tuck the envelope into his inside pocket, she understood.

The next day as she walked to work, she started to think about breaking it off with Irving. Her job was done, but, of course, Irving didn't know she'd been using him, and he'd summoned up all his courage and asked her out to the movies. She'd politely declined, claiming she needed to spend more time with Max, which was true. Her son was the love of her life. Isn't that why she was doing this in the first place? She'd just have to tell Irving she wasn't ready for a relationship—the mourning period for Jews usually lasted a year anyway. She was practicing what to tell him when a strange sensation came over her.

Someone was following her.

She turned around and saw a black sedan, crawling along 57th Street a few yards behind her. Her gaze went to the license plate, which was supposed to be bolted to the fender, but there was none. Adrenaline flooded through her, and every sense went on alert. She tried to remember what Hans had told her about losing a tail. Fortunately, an alley lay just ahead. She ducked into it, then spun around to get a look at the car and driver. The driver, a man, was wearing a straw boater and sunglasses, which effectively disguised his face. Yet there was something familiar about him. The set of his head. The shape of his face. Still, she couldn't place him. She stared after the sedan, but it turned right at the next corner and disappeared.

CHAPTER 21

August-September, 1942

In August some of the physicists at Met Lab isolated a microscopic amount of plutonium. It was a major development; the entire department buzzed with the news. This meant that it *was* possible to separate plutonium from uranium and thus produce a supply of it for the bomb. Met Lab was on the right track. In the meantime, Enrico Fermi and his team continued with experiments that would produce a chain reaction in the Pile.

Lena fed the information to Hans. He'd been elated with her sketch of the Pile, and he seemed fascinated by every new development. She also passed him the news that construction of the bomb and its materials would not be in Chicago. Production would relocate to the Clinch River in Tennessee and would be turned over to a private firm reporting to the Army. An experimental pile would be built in the Argonne Forest Preserve just outside Chicago, but the Met Lab scientists were just that, scientists and researchers, not facility operators. Compton had wanted to keep everything at the University, she told Hans, but he was overruled. People were fearful of an accident in such a heavily populated area.

In September, the Army appointed Colonel Leslie R. Groves to head the production effort, which was now called the Manhattan Project. Groves, a former West Pointer with the Army Corps of Engineers, had supervised the construction of the Pentagon building in Washington. When Groves took command, he made it clear that by the end of the year, a decision would be made as to which process would be used to produce a bomb.

Lena dutifully reported the news to Hans. Occasionally Hans would meet her in a black Ford, and they'd drive around the South Side. Other times they met in a coffee shop, always a different one. This time he drove to a diner where they sat at the counter. A fresh-faced boy with a white peaked cap took their order of iced tea for Lena, a chocolate milkshake for Hans. Leaning her elbows on the counter, Lena watched the boy make the milkshake.

"Do you have another car, a black sedan of some sort?" she asked.

Hans frowned. It took him a moment to reply. He shook his head. "No. Why?"

"Someone was following me in a black car. I did not know the make."

"When?"

"Perhaps a week or so ago."

"Where?"

"On 57th Street. In the morning. I was on my way to work."

Hans arched his eyebrows. "Did you see who it was?"

She shook her head. "He was wearing sunglasses and a boater."

Hans splayed his hands on the counter. "I have no idea."

Lena looked over. "The man looked familiar. But I couldn't place him."

Hans shrugged. "Perhaps he just wanted to follow an attractive woman." He smiled, but it looked forced.

The boy behind the counter brought their drinks. Lena reached for a straw and sipped her tea. Hans hadn't made the slightest move towards her in the months they'd been working together. He'd been totally professional, although he clearly knew she'd been using her womanly charms on Irving. For a moment she wondered why he kept her at a distance, especially when he told her more than once how attractive she was. Then she decided it was better this way. Not only was he a Nazi, but any undue attention from him would give her something else to worry about.

CHAPTER 22

———

Lena was at work one evening in late September. The door to the Department was closed, but a breeze with just a hint of fall wafted through a window. She was glad summer was over; the heat and humidity had seemed particularly harsh this year. She'd just finished photographing the latest batch of letters and documents and was putting the originals back into the file cabinet when she felt a draft. She spun around.

A man in an army uniform stood at the door to the Department, his gaze locked on her. The stripes on his shoulders said he was an officer. He had short bristly gray hair, pale blue eyes that were a touch rheumy. Frown lines etched across his forehead. He'd once been fit, she thought, but a large belly indicated those days were over. In the short sleeves of his summer uniform, his arms and the back of his hands were covered with heavy dark hair, which gave him a slightly simian look.

Lena froze. How long had he been there? Why hadn't she heard the door open? What had he seen? Panic crawled up her spine. Her arms and legs felt like they had suddenly detached from her body.

The man folded his arms. "And just what are you doing, young lady?"

The blood left her head in a rush. She wanted to look down to see if her hands were shaking but she didn't dare. This was it. She had been caught. Then she recalled one of Hans' rules of tradecraft. If she was ever cornered or caught, the best defense was a good offense. She'd told Hans at the time she didn't know if she could. He'd chuckled and said, "You will. You'll see."

Now, she realized he was right. There was no other option. She drew herself up, not sure where her courage was coming from. "I should be asking the same of you."

The officer's brows shot up. "Do you know who I am?"

Lena mustered what she hoped was an intimidating scowl. "I have no idea. So I will call security. This is a protected facility." She started toward the telephone on her desk.

He took a step forward. "I am Colonel Charles Collins."

Lena continued to her desk and slipped behind it. Her purse was on the floor, and as she got to it, she unobtrusively kicked it further under the desk. Then she lifted her gaze, as if she'd just made the connection. "Collins? You were here a few years ago."

"I was. And now I'm back." His expression bordered on arrogance. "Who are you?"

She eyed him warily. A wave of trepidation rolled through her, but she was damned if she'd let him see it. "The Department is closed, Colonel. In fact, I am obligated to report your unauthorized visit. How did you get this far? Our security is first-rate."

"Whoever you are, you clearly do not know my position."

"And you do not know mine." Lena was amazed

at herself. Where had she acquired this steely resolve? She opened her drawer, took out paper and pen, and wrote his name down. "A report will be filed tomorrow morning."

"And to whom do you think the reports go?"

She looked him up and down, wondering if he could smell the fear on her.

"I am in charge of security. My job is to ensure there are no breaches at the Met Lab. Now. You either tell me who you are or I will have you detained."

Lena didn't know whether to believe him or not, but in case he was telling the truth, she answered. "I am Lena Stern, one of the secretaries for the Department." She hesitated. "And if what you are saying is true, why was I not told about you?" It felt like a bird was fluttering inside her stomach.

"Obviously your security clearance level is not high enough," he said.

The stress coupled with his self-importance made her want to let out a nervous laugh. She pressed her lips together so she wouldn't.

"Why are you here?" he repeated.

She parried the question. "If you are who you say you are, you would know."

He stared at her, his face reddening.

"There is so much work these days that I occasionally stay late to catch up." She bent down and reached for her purse, hoping he wouldn't spot the Minox lying on top. "But now if you'll excuse me, Colonel..." She snapped the clasp of her purse shut. "...I am going home."

She felt his eyes on her back as she walked out the door.

CHAPTER 23

———————

Collins became a ubiquitous, unwanted presence in the department. He was intrusive, especially to those below his rank, which was almost everyone, since most of the scientists were civilians. But the Army had been put back in charge of the Manhattan Project, and Collins was free to meddle. Every day he demanded clearances, records, documents, and memos, disrupting both Lena and Sonia's workload. They understood the importance of security, but Collins used it as a cudgel to force his way into situations. The only person who could control him was Compton, but he was preoccupied by meetings with top army and government officials and wasn't around much. Most of the staff came to loathe Collins.

Because of him, Lena told Hans she'd have to slow down for a while. It was too risky. Hans agreed. Lena was happy to leave work at a reasonable time for a change, and spent more time with Max. He was three and a half now, and a curious child. He asked questions all the time, and Lena found herself studying how birds flew, how clouds formed, and why leaves turned colors.

Meanwhile Irving continued to be worrisome. Lena hadn't had the heart to tell him they were through. Still, she did cut down on the time she spent with him, and she could tell he was growing frustrated. She worried about how he'd react when she told him it was over.

* * *

The crisis came in October. Lena had just put Max down for the night when the buzzer sounded. She pressed the intercom button, and a crisp voice said, "This is Colonel Collins."

Lena's knees buckled. Why was he here? Had he discovered proof of her treason? Was this the knock on her door in the middle of the night? She feared the worst. Still, she'd learned to be on the offense with him. "Colonel," she said sharply. "It's late. I'm just about to retire for the night."

He cleared his throat. "I have urgent business to discuss."

Her throat closed up. What should she do? His voice cut in. "Please, Mrs. Stern."

She drew back. He sounded almost polite. Could it possibly be about something other than her espionage? She took a breath and buzzed him in.

When she opened the door, she saw he was still in uniform, but it was wrinkled and creased as if he'd been rolling around on the floor. His face was pale as well. Normally, he had a too ruddy look. She smelled alcohol on him.

"Thank you for seeing me," he said.

She gave him a cautious nod. "Come in, Colonel. But please keep your voice down. My son is asleep."

He stepped in and looked around. Lena's natural civility kicked in.

"Would you like a glass of water?"

"You got anything stronger?"

Surprised at the request, she stammered,

"I—I—might." She went into the kitchen and rummaged through a cabinet. Irving had brought over some whiskey a few months earlier. She found it behind the canisters of flour and sugar. It was nearly full. About to ask him how he took it, she turned around and suddenly started. Collins was standing in the doorway to the kitchen. She hadn't heard him approach. She jumped back. This is it, she thought. I am *gefickt*.

He held up his hand. "I'm sorry. I didn't mean to frighten you."

She let out a breath, trying to suppress her fear. "How—how do you take it? The whiskey, I mean?"

"Straight. Just a glass."

She got one out, filled it halfway, and handed it to him. They headed back to the living room. Lena sat in the chair, leaving him the sofa. She laced her hands together.

He sat down and took a long pull on the drink.

"What's so important, Colonel?" She tried to keep the edge out of her voice, but she was still nervous.

"I have a proposition for you."

Her eyebrows went up. If this was a

confrontation, it was a strange way to begin. She sat up straighter.

"I know you are seeing one of the physicists in the department."

She stiffened.

"Irving Mandell. Don't deny it. Several sources have confirmed it."

"Colonel," Lena said in a cool voice. "You know how tongues wag and rumors begin. Usually they are greatly exaggerated. I lost my husband ten months ago. I am still in mourning."

"Are you saying it isn't true, Mrs. Stern?"

Lena couldn't resist. "It is not. But even if it was, what business is it of yours?"

"Mandell's business is very much my business, Mrs. Stern. We believe," he cleared his throat, "that he is spying for a foreign government."

Lena froze. Irving? A spy? She sagged against the chair. How had they come to that conclusion? Or was this a trap? Was Collins accusing Irving, hoping that Lena would defend him and blurt out the truth? She had to be careful.

"That is impossible," she finally said. "Irving is one of the most loyal, patriotic people I know." She paused. "What makes you believe he isn't?"

"You know I can't divulge that. It's classified."

Of course it was, she thought. In some ways, with his visits after dark, his innuendo and interrogation techniques, this American was not so different from a Nazi. But what about the substance of his remarks? It's the Pile, she decided. Someone knows they were there. But why would he single out Irving and not her too?

"Mrs. Stern." He took another long drink. "You can deny it all you want, but I know the two of you are seeing each other. I have photos of you together. At a restaurant just off campus."

Stunned, Lena sat up straight. "You've been following us? And you have photos?" Her voice rose an octave. She was unsure whether to be terrified or furious.

Collins raised a finger to his lips. "You might want to lower your voice. Didn't you say your son was sleeping?" His mouth curled into a tiny smile of triumph.

Lena went mute. All she could do was glare.

He pointed his finger. "You see, Mrs. Stern, you're right about one thing. I don't care about the nature of your relationship. If the two of you are fucking like rabbits, that's your choice. What I do care about is the security of the Met Lab. And for that, I need your help."

Lena kept her mouth shut. She was afraid even to blink, for fear she would reveal something she shouldn't.

"In fact, I want you to keep your courtship going. See him as much as you can. Deepen your relationship." He couldn't resist a smile. "On one condition, of course. You will report back to me. Let me know everything he is doing. At work and at play. I need evidence."

"You want me to spy on my co-worker."

"Plural," he said.

"What are you talking about?"

"Mandell is number one on my list. But there are others. I want you to be my eyes and ears when I'm not around. Anything you find that is top secret. Anything that will give us intel on our enemies."

Lena inclined her head. "Intel?"

He nodded. "Is that going to be a problem?"

Nausea climbed up Lena's throat. Things had gone far enough. "I will not do it. Irving is the farthest thing from a spy. He would never betray his country. Or his colleagues. He is proud to be an

American. So are the others in the department. I will not stoop to your level."

"I'm glad you brought up the term 'American,' Mrs. Stern," Collins said. "I have studied your background as well. I know you are a refugee from Germany. And a Jew."

There was just the slightest emphasis on the word "Jew."

"I am an American citizen. My husband worked at Met Lab. That is where we met."

"I am aware of that." He waved a hand. "But in this environment, in these times, one never knows who is a friend and who is an enemy. If you do not cooperate, your life—and that of your son could become—well—difficult."

"Are you threatening me, Colonel?" Lena said. She was shaking with rage now, not fear.

"Not at all, Mrs. Stern. Just reminding you of your duty as an American. Especially during a war in which enemies are all around us. Think it over."

CHAPTER 24

———

Lena couldn't sleep. She went to the kitchen, poured some of the whiskey she'd given Collins, and tossed it down. She had to tell Irving that Collins suspected him of espionage, but how could she do that without exposing herself? For all she knew, that was Collins' plan all along. He'd never liked her, and now he had a good reason to keep a close eye on her through Irving.

She was now going to be exploited by two groups, each for their own purposes. It didn't matter that Collins was clumsier and less sophisticated than the Germans. To both groups she was nothing more than a pawn, an insignificant player on a complicated chessboard. What would they do to her when she had served her purpose? What would they do to Max?

She covered her face with her hands. She was approaching a point of no return. Her days as a spy—perhaps even life itself—were numbered. How had it come to this? Maybe she should have stayed in Germany with her family and Josef. She would undoubtedly be dead by now, but at least it would have been a honorable death. Unsullied by shame or scandal.

She paced back and forth in the living room. There might be someone whose help she could enlist. He'd been the one person—the only person—to suggest a connection between events. She had no reason to think he would help her; he might throw her to the wolves, like the others surely would. And if he did help, life would become more difficult. She tried to brainstorm other options, but she didn't see any.

She rummaged around the apartment for his card. He'd given it to her months earlier. She searched the kitchen, then the bedroom, but couldn't find it. She grew more frantic. She had to find it. She finally saw it in her jewelry box on the dresser. She grabbed it and practically ran to the telephone.

When he answered, she said breathlessly, "This is Lena Stern. You helped when my husband Karl—was—died. And then when my son was kidnapped."

"Hello, Lena," Agent Lanier said. "I've been waiting for your call."

CHAPTER 25

The following morning ushered in a crisp fall day, the kind that evoked thoughts of a sweet new year filled with apples and honey. The High Holidays had come and gone—they'd been early this year—but the swirl of scarlet, yellow, and orange leaves outside was a reminder of the season. Lena gave Max extra hugs before leaving for work.

She was under strict instructions not to tell Hans or Collins about her conversation with Lanier. He had come over after she called, and sat, ironically, in the same spot on the sofa as Collins. She told him everything. Then they discussed her options.

"I want you to work for us."

"Us?"

"The United States."

"I thought I already was. Through Collins."

"We haven't been able to pin him down. He may be a rogue agent, working for himself because he wasn't formally assigned to Manhattan. Or maybe he's something else. We just don't know."

"What do you want me to do?"

"Essentially, we want you to mix up your intel. Put misleading information in some of the documents you pass to Hans. Collins too. Things that either mean nothing or are outright lies."

Lena bit her lip, thinking back to the sketch of the Pile she'd altered. She told Lanier about it.

"Exactly. Good work. That's what we want."

"But how? How will I figure out what is meaningful and what isn't?"

"I'll let you know. I'll take a look at everything you're planning to pass. A day won't make much difference. You'll have to make sure I get a copy of everything before you send it on."

"How will I get it to you?"

"How do you do it now?"

She told him.

He nodded. "We'll set up our own dead drop."

She ran a hand through her hair. "What happens when they realize the documents have been adulterated?"

"They won't," he paused, "if you're careful. Remember, you're going to be passing them genuine intel also."

"To Collins too, you say?"

Lanier nodded. "At this point, it's better to be safe than sorry, don't you agree?"

Lena didn't reply.

"Hey. I'm gonna do my best to back you up. You're working for the good guys now."

Skeptical, she flashed him a look.

"Okay." He shifted. She could smell his aftershave. "Now, let's talk about tomorrow."

* * *

Lena had two tasks. One, she was to tell Hans that Irving was now suspected of spying himself, and it was her fault. She would ask Hans what he could do to manage the situation. She would also talk about winding down her work. She would tell him she was prepared for the consequences, but she had to be honest; she was slowly going mad with guilt. Two, she would tell Irving about Collins' visit. He deserved to know he was under surveillance, she would say. Perhaps together they could come up with a solution to the Colonel's scheming.

She wanted to talk to Irving right away, but she had to wait; he usually dropped by around lunchtime. Today, though, lunchtime came and went without him. Lena asked Sonia if she'd seen him. Sonia shook her head.

"But I have something to tell you."

Lena felt her stomach twist.

"I finally heard from Frank," Sonia grinned. "He's all right. He'll be coming home in a couple of months." Sonia's husband had been drafted and fought the Battle of Midway over the summer, but Sonia hadn't heard from him in weeks.

A wave of relief so profound it came out as a gasp swept over Lena. "That's wonderful, Sonia. Congratulations!" She pasted on a smile and hoped it looked genuine.

"There's something else." Sonia tilted her head. "Once he's home, I—I won't be coming back."

"Oh, no." Lena realized she had become fond of the girl. Not to mention that whoever replaced her might be a plant. She squeezed her eyes shut. She despised having to think this way.

"I am not as dedicated as you, Lena," Sonia added. "I could never spend all the time at work that you do." Dedicated? Is that what Sonia thought? Lena bit back a reply. She didn't want to spoil Sonia's joy.

* * *

Lena went to a pay phone after lunch and made a call.

"Where have you been, Irving? I've been so worried."

"I was fired."

"What? Why?"

"Collins knows I was in the Pile when I wasn't supposed to be. The guard told him he heard two people. He didn't know the other, but he thought it was a woman. Collins thinks I'm a spy. He says he'll keep it under wraps if I go quietly."

"That's impossible. A spy? For whom?" Lena asked. She couldn't help wondering whether Collins knew the truth about *her*. Had he put the pieces together? Had his night visit been nothing but a ruse after all?

"For the Communists."

"The Communists? Wherever would he get that idea?" Inwardly, though, she let out a breath. She'd been handed a reprieve. Collins wasn't focusing on Nazi espionage. But her relief soon turned into self-loathing. How could she be thankful that the Nazis were off the hook?

"Irving?" There was no response. "Irving, we need to talk. This is all my fault."

Silence on his end. He wasn't disagreeing.

"Irving," she said, "I'm going to tell Collins I was the one who wanted to go in. If anything, I should be the one who's fired."

This time he answered. "No. There's no sense both of us suffering."

She hoped he'd say that. "But I can't let you take the blame when it was my idea." She pondered whether there really *was* any way to salvage the situation. Could she actually try to convince Collins that Irving was innocent? That it had been just an adventure? No. He'd never believe her. He'd either think she was defending Irving, or he'd focus his suspicions on her. He probably had already. Then again, what did it matter? It was just a matter of time until she was exposed by Hans, Collins, perhaps even Lanier.

"No." Irving was firm. "You can't lose your job. I know how much you depend on it." He paused. "But I do have a question. Why did you want to see the Pile so badly? Is there something I should know?"

Mein Gott. Lena stared at a sign for the dry cleaners across the street, but all she saw was a blurry mass of letters. She must not be a very good spy if her supposed boyfriend distrusted her. She wanted to melt into the ground, like that witch in the movie about Dorothy and the Wizard. She answered carefully.

"Irving, you know me. What do you think?"

A long pause followed. Then, "I'm sorry, Lena. It's just this—all of this—is so alien to my whole being. My parents said I could move back in with them. But how can I? It—it would be admitting failure. If I can't work at Met Lab, I don't know what I'll do."

"You are not a spy, Irving. We both know it." She continued in a rush, grasping for something to say. "For all we know, Collins may be anti-Semitic. It wouldn't be surprising."

He sighed. "Anti-Jew Pro-Jew, who cares? It could be anyone... Sonia... you... me... even Compton, for Christ's sake. A cloud of suspicion can fall on anyone these days."

"Irving, stop!" What had she done to this wonderful young man? He was a shadow of what he had once been. A despondent, sad shadow. And it was her doing.

"Lena, I want to see you tonight. Please. Can I come over?"

She covered her eyes with one hand. She was meeting Hans that evening. She couldn't risk the two running into each other. She was just about to suggest the next night instead when he cut in.

"I understand." He'd mistaken the silence as her answer. "Goodbye, Lena."

"No, wait, Irving. That's not—"

But he'd hung up.

CHAPTER 26

———

Lena went through the next few hours like one of those zombies in a Bela Lugosi horror film. During the meeting with Hans in a coffee shop, she told him about Irving, how she'd been using him to get the sketch of the Pile, and how it had backfired.

"You have to do something," she said, her voice full of anguish.

Hans shrugged.

"Please. I'm begging you."

"You are sure he doesn't know anything?"

She looked down, recalling Irving's question about whether there was anything he should know about her.

"What is it, Lena?" Hans sounded irritated.

She looked up. "He doesn't know anything. I'm sure of it."

"I see." Hans' eyes narrowed. She knew he didn't believe her.

* * *

Lena was surprised that no one at work talked about Irving. Or at least they didn't talk to her about him. She supposed people knew they'd been seeing each other and weren't sure what Lena's feelings were. In a way it was a blessing. She tried to concentrate on her work, but every time Collins came in, he'd stop to ask if she had any news, or make a comment that meant hurry up and get me something. She started to bite her nails, something she'd never done before. Headaches came and went. She lost her appetite, and had trouble sleeping. Even Max couldn't chase away her bad moods.

A week later, towards the end of October, Lena came into work early, ostensibly to catch up on paperwork. She thought about photographing a letter or two, but decided it was too risky. She never knew when Collins would show up.

It was a good decision; twenty minutes later Collins swept into the office. His usual bluster wasn't apparent; in fact, his facial muscles were stretched taut and his eyes radiated distress.

"Did you hear?"

Lena's pulse sped up. Collins rarely brought good news.

"There's been a terrible fire."

Lena jumped out of her chair, ran to a window, and looked out. No flames. No smell of smoke. "Where? I don't see anything." She turned around.

"Not here." He planted his hands on his hips. "Are you sure you haven't heard?"

"Colonel, I have no idea what you're talking about." Her heart pounded in her chest. "What—where is it?"

He paused for just a fraction of a second, then said, "Your beau. Irving Mandell. His parents' home burned down last night."

"Oh, *Mein Gott!*" Lena screamed. Her hands flew to the sides of her head.

"The fire department said a Halloween candle in the window somehow ignited the curtains beside it."

"But—but—" She sputtered. "That cannot be."

Irving and his parents didn't celebrate Halloween. Irving had told Lena more than once that his family was observant. They would have considered Halloween a pagan ritual. Someone had deliberately set the fire and covered it up.

Collins went on. "Luckily, Mr. and Mrs. Mandell were not at home." He cleared his throat. "But Irving was."

Lena started to pull at her hair.

"He didn't make it, Mrs. Stern. He's gone."

* * *

It didn't take long for the staff at Met Lab to start discussing the cause of the fire. Shock and horror quickly led to discussions about Irving, the abrupt end to his career, the rumors about espionage. Lena wasn't sure who first speculated that his death might not have been an accident. That Irving, morose and despondent at losing his job, had set it himself. Others pointed a finger at Collins and wanted him fired. They were sure Collins had somehow "arranged" the accident.

Lena knew better. Irving was distraught and depressed, but he would never have killed himself. And Collins didn't have the guts to make someone disappear. He was a bad man, a fount of fear and suspicion, but he wasn't a killer.

She knew who had set the fire. And why. And with that knowledge, the last bit of her composure snapped. The situation was out of control. She had to protect Max. And herself. No matter what.

The following Saturday morning Lena told Mrs. M she had an errand to run and asked Mrs. M to look after Max. She took the bus over to Chinatown, got off at Cermak and Wentworth and headed south. At the corner of 23rd Street, she turned right. Chen's Gun and Surplus occupied a shop in the middle of the block. Lena pushed through the door. Thirty minutes later she left with a Smith and Wesson .38 revolver and a box of bullets.

CHAPTER 27

November, 1942

Lena didn't know how she got through the month of November. Spying for both Hans and Collins, and reporting to Lanier as well, was nearly an impossible balancing act. And it was a performance—for Hans, Collins, even for Lanier. She felt like an actor playing three roles, and she had to keep track of what she said to whom. If she dropped just one line to the wrong player, she would be exposed, even possibly killed, faster than Superman's speeding bullet.

At least with Hans, she didn't have to worry about a physical copy of the intelligence she passed, genuine or not; the film from the Minox was a lifesaver. But Collins and Lanier required actual documents. She normally used carbon paper for the copies she typed, so she added two more sheets, but when the copies weren't perfectly aligned, they jammed in the roller and looked messy. Occasionally Lena would glance over at Sonia, afraid that that the girl would see what she was doing, but Sonia was preoccupied with her husband's return and seemed oblivious.

Incoming letters and memos had to be copied by hand. She started to sneak documents into her bag to take home to copy once Max was asleep. She was careful to disguise her penmanship, in case someone from the department might link it to her. Of course, it was easier to alter the documents that way. But there was also the problem of passing the materials. Collins maintained he had a top security clearance. But when she asked Lanier, he'd told her the man was lying. Still, she had no choice. She had to deliver the intel.

The first piece she passed Collins was a letter from Compton to the Army with an analysis of the latest news from Berkeley, California. J. Robert Oppenheimer was supervising the work of a group of theoretical physicists that included Felix Bloch, Hans Bethe, Edward Teller, Robert Serber, and John H. Manley from Chicago's Met Lab. The group decided they would need twice as much fissionable material as they'd previously estimated to build the bomb. In a letter Compton had reserved judgment until the Pile yielded results.

At lunchtime Lena folded the letter, threw on her coat and gloves, and told Sonia she was going for a walk. Before going downstairs, she stopped in the ladies room and slipped the copy of the letter inside one of her gloves. Outside, she bumped into Collins as they'd planned, and casually dropped the glove on the ground. Collins bent over and picked it up.

That afternoon, he showed up in the office. "Ladies." He waved a red glove in Sonia and Lena's direction. "Do you have any idea who this belongs to? I found it outside."

Sonia looked over at Lena. "Isn't that part of the pair you just bought, Lena?"

Lena looked up in surprise. "Why, yes. It is. Thank you, Colonel. I must have dropped it when I went to lunch."

* * *

That night Lena stayed late to finish her work. She had just put on her coat to leave when Collins appeared at the door. She hated how he seemed to slip in and out of the shadows.

He flashed her a suspicious look. "How did you know I want intel on Oppenheimer?"

She shook her head. "I didn't."

His eyebrows arched.

"Colonel, I assume you want any information on the Manhattan Project that seems relevant. And to which you are not otherwise privy," she couldn't help adding.

He stiffened. "Well then," he cleared his throat, "Fate has intervened. I want whatever you can find on Oppenheimer. What he thinks, what he does, how much money he has, what he spends it on. When he takes a shower or cheats on his wife. Anything and everything."

Lena didn't reply.

"You know who he is," Collins went on.

"He's a colleague of Professor Compton's and a brilliant physicist."

"He is also known to associate with Communists, and we have a strong suspicion he is one himself. In fact, he is the reason I'm here. This man may well become the leader of the Manhattan Project when construction begins. We must keep a close eye on him." He paused. "Good work."

Lena walked home slowly. She couldn't do it any more. This was insanity. She would certainly be exposed and the retribution, from the Nazis or Collins or even Lanier, would ruin her. It had to end, one way or another, despite what the three men wanted. Fortunately, she had an idea how to stir things up, perhaps push events towards a speedy conclusion. When she got home she signaled for a meeting with Hans.

CHAPTER 28

———

"There's been a complication," she told Hans when they met the next day.

"What?" Hans asked.

She told him about Collins. "I wanted to tell you before, but I have been afraid. I do not know how much he knows about my—our—situation. I wanted to be sure before I came to you."

Hans' face was unreadable. "What have you been passing to him?"

"Pretty much the same thing I've given you."

Hans grunted. "Make sure you tell me exactly what material he gets from now on." He appraised her. "Does he have any idea about our arrangement?"

"That's why I waited. He does not know. I am sure."

She expected Hans to be suspicious, to threaten reprisals, to punish her in some way. To her surprise, though, he smiled. "Well, well, this could actually be quite useful. Make sure you continue to update me on him."

Update him? That was all? Lena tensed. Hans really did seem unconcerned. But they'd had Irving killed for getting in the way. Her plan wasn't working. "How can you say Collins *might* be useful? He's a serious threat."

"What makes you believe that?"

Lena felt her anger build. "Hans, look at the situation. You have me spying for the Germans. Collins has me spying on the Communists. If he finds out, I am finished. Especially now that Hitler has invaded Russia."

"Lena, do not worry."

He was trying to soothe her. Badly, she thought. "You seem to forget it is my life at stake."

"You are doing a wonderful job."

She took a deep breath. "No. This cannot

continue. I want out. That's why I told you about Collins. It has become too dangerous. I cannot do this anymore. *Genuch ist genuch.*"

Hans nodded. "I understand. It will not be long now."

"What do you mean?"

"We all know that when construction begins, the Manhattan Project will relocate to other places. You will, of course, remain here. The only question is when the move will take place. We will reassess your options at that point."

"But what about Collins? What are you going to do about him?"

Hans seemed unperturbed. "Nothing. He's—what do the Americans say? 'Small potatoes.'"

Lena knew she would go straight to hell for thinking it, but she couldn't wait for the bomb to be built. At least she would be free.

If she was still alive.

CHAPTER 29

_____

December, 1942

The moment everyone at Met Lab had been working toward happened at 3:30 PM on Wednesday, December 2. One of Fermi's assistants moved the last control rod into place, and at 3:25, the core began to feed on itself. At 3:30, Chicago Pile #1, the mountain of graphite, uranium metal, and uranium oxide, produced the first self-sustaining nuclear chain reaction. The power level was only half a watt, but nobody cared. The reactor worked!

Compton immediately called James Conant, the National Defense Research Committee Chairman, and, speaking in code, said, "the Italian navigator has just landed in the new world."

"Were the natives friendly?" Conant asked.

"Everyone landed safe and happy."

* * *

The celebration at a nearby bar was long-lived and raucous, if a group of physicists could be called raucous. No one was happier than Lena. The next phase of the bomb's development would begin, but her work would end. She couldn't wait. She was going to quit her job and find something completely different: a position at an insurance company or a manufacturing plant. She'd had enough of science she didn't understand, as well as the duplicity she understood too well. The money would be a loss, but the chance to regain her self-respect would more than make up for it.

Over the next few days, Met Lab scientists raised the power inside the Pile to two hundred watts to make sure the chain reaction hadn't been a fluke. That afternoon one of the scientists came out of the Pile with burns on his arms. Lena didn't say anything, but she knew that radiation, a byproduct of the chain reaction, was dangerous. Three days later, that scientist became ill; by the end of the week he was dead. It was a devastating blow. In a way Lena was glad Irving was no longer with them. He would have died for the Manhattan project, too. In fact, he had.

CHAPTER 30

———

A few days later, Lena was filing a top-secret memo to Compton from Groves. In her impatience to photograph it, she almost missed it, but the word "Germany" drew her attention. Groves reported something they'd suspected and now had confirmed. The Germans had given up serious atomic research at least a year earlier. Possibly more. Hitler simply did not have the resources or manpower to experiment. Finances were a huge drain now that the Nazis were fighting a two-front war. Every available *Reich mark* had been allocated to the *Wehrmacht*.

Lena's eyes widened. For the past six months

she, like everyone else at Met Lab, believed Nazi Germany was an existential threat to America. That German scientists were working furiously on atomic weapons development, and, in fact, were ahead of the US. Now, it appeared the opposite was the truth. What she and everyone else had been told was just propaganda. Lies. A way, perhaps, to get the Americans to work longer, harder, faster.

She finished photographing the memo on her Minox and slipped it into the dead drop on the way home. She knew it would trigger a reaction. She was ostensibly spying for the Germans. The same Germans who were *not* working on an atom bomb. So if the Germans weren't making a bomb, why was she spying for them? True, they might want information anyway, but why the urgency? The cloak and dagger meetings and signals? Moreover, if the Germans were designating every mark for the *Wehrmacht*, where did the money she'd been given come from?

She thought back over the events of the past year, starting with Karl's death last December. A death that had never been resolved. Then Max's kidnapping in April, which had not been solved either. Irving died in a mysterious fire that

October, after she'd made him show her the Pile. Three tragic events in twelve months. They weren't all coincidence. She'd known that, deep within her subconscious, but she hadn't wanted to admit it.

But now she had to. Her survival depended on it. Hans and his Nazi companions had orchestrated everything. Killing Karl was the first step. It made her penniless and vulnerable. Then they abducted Max, returning him only when she agreed to work for them. Finally, they got rid of Irving—he was a complication they didn't need.

And now they would be closing in on her. When they figured out she knew it had all been a ruse, what would they do? She recalled how vague Hans had been about her future once the Manhattan Project moved. What if she had no future? What if she was nothing more than a pawn in their operation? Unimportant. Expendable.

A wave of hot emotion rolled over her. She explored it. Tasted it. For once it wasn't fear. It was anger. An anger approaching fury. After everything that had been done to her and her loved ones, how could she let them make her superfluous?

When she got home, she fixed dinner, then played Lincoln Logs with Max until bedtime. Once he was asleep, she tried to come up with a plan. She could go to Collins and confess she was a double. Expose Hans and his people. But Collins had never trusted her, despite the fact she was passing him intelligence. He would accuse her of treason, and he'd be right. He wouldn't understand the desperation of a mother forced to protect her child. She would certainly spend the rest of her life in prison. She might even be executed.

She slumped on the sofa, head in her hands. Lanier was no guarantee of safe passage, either. He'd hadn't made any promises. He'd simply said that, in return for her compliance, he would try to "back her up." She was truly *gefickt*.

She went to the closet and retrieved the .38. She brought it back to the living room, and raised it in the air. Then she aimed it an imaginary target. Could she do it for real? Her throat closed up. She wasn't sure. All she knew is they would not—could not win. Not this time. She knew something else too. Her days as a spy were at an end. No more deception. No more duplicity.

She picked up the phone.

CHAPTER 31

December, 1942

The next day Lena spotted the signal from Hans on her way back from lunch with Sonia. A miniature American flag stood in a snow-covered urn in front of the 57th Street florist. He wanted to meet her after work. She considered not showing up. But if she didn't, Hans would come after her, or worse, Max. So when she got home, she went to the closet, loaded the .38 and slipped it into her coat pocket. At least she would have the element of surprise.

The Ford rolled up a few minutes later. A typical winter day in Chicago, the sun was setting, but it had snowed a few inches the night before, and the bite in the air required gloves, hats, and scarves. Lena waited until the car stopped and the window rolled down.

Hans called out from the driver's seat. "Come in and get warm."

Only after she slid into the passenger seat did she realize another man was in back. She turned around to take a look. He was a beefy, muscled bull of a man. That chilled her more than the frigid December weather.

"Who is this?" She asked.

Hans waved a hand. "This is Dieter."

The man looked up at the mention of his name.

"He doesn't speak English," Hans said.

"Why is he here?"

"I'm training him," Hans said, but the pause before he spoke told her that was a lie.

Lena's thoughts darkened. Dieter had to be an assassin, and she was his target. He was there to "deal" with her. She bit her lip. She briefly thought of escaping. Throwing herself out of the car. The Ford was heading south on Lake Shore Drive. But timing was everything. She'd have to scoot to the edge of the seat, fling open the car door, and propel herself onto the road. And she'd have to make sure other traffic was far enough behind that she wouldn't be run over. She let out a frustrated breath. There were too many variables. She couldn't do it.

She hoped Hans would turn in at one of the beaches along the Drive. Maybe then she could make her move. Sure enough, at 77th Street, Hans turned into Rainbow Beach and Park, a peninsula that jutted out onto the lake. A wide expanse of lawn with picnic tables and a sandy beach beyond, it was always crowded in summer. She and Karl had come here to admire the view of the Loop to the north, which on sunny summer days was so spectacular it should have been on one of those picture postcards. Now, though, with its skeletal tree branches, grass that was brown and brittle and covered with snow, the park was as empty and desolate as an abandoned graveyard.

"Why are we here?" Lena asked.

"We wanted a place where we wouldn't be interrupted. You have been asking questions. It's time to give you some answers."

She stole a glance at Hans. What game was he playing? The only answer she expected was a loaded pistol aimed at her. Hans pulled around a graceful drive that led to a squat building bordering the lake and parked. He switched off the ignition and motioned for her to open the door.

"Now we walk."

They got out of the car and started across the park away from the lake. Hans and Dieter flanked her. Dusk plunged the park into shadows, which softened the definition of objects, making them difficult to identify. She slipped her hands in her pockets, felt the comforting weight of her revolver. At least she wasn't without some defense.

Beyond a stand of trees was a picnic table covered with a layer of snow. As they approached, a figure emerged from the gloom. A man wrapped up in what looked like a black Chesterfield coat, a black fedora on his head, sturdy boots on his feet. Something was familiar about him. The shape of his head. The sharp edge of his chin. The lift of his shoulders. Lena's heart banged in her chest. She knew this man. She quickened her pace.

He studied her as she approached, his body angled toward hers in a way she remembered well. As she closed in, he gave her a smile.

Lena sucked in a breath. "Josef!"

CHAPTER 32

———

Josef's smile widened. "Hello, Lena."

Lena had forgotten her boots, and enough snow had seeped into her shoes to make her shiver. But the block of ice in her heart made her feet feel hot. "I—I do not understand. What are you doing here?"

He extended his hands, which were encased in thick leather gloves. "I am here for you."

"For me?" Lena blinked in a daze of confusion. "What do you mean? How long have you been in America?"

"Long enough."

"Why did you not contact me?"

He paused. "I did. Through Hans. I have known every move you've made."

"But you were in Budapest. How did you—"

A trace of irritation unfolded across his face. "You never used to be this slow, Lena. Hans mentioned how tentative you have become. Now I see he was right. "

Lena scowled.

He paused and took a breath. When he spoke again his tone was conciliatory. "I'm sorry. I know how much you've been through. It would make anyone uncertain."

Lena took a good look at him. Josef seemed older; she thought she spotted a touch of gray at his temples. But he was still tall. And strong. With the Aryan look that had always made her feel part proud, part ashamed. He was watching her with an expectant expression, and she realized she was supposed to say something.

"How—how did you find me? We haven't been in touch."

"Oh, Lena," he spread his hands. "Think. It is quite simple."

She squinted in concentration. When it came to her, she took a few steps back, and her mouth dropped open. "You! You've been directing the operation."

He dipped his head in acknowledgement.

"But—but..." she sputtered. "... How? Why? You are a Jew."

He shrugged.

A streak of fury shot up her spine. "You passed, didn't you?" she hissed. She recalled how they had joked years ago that with his blond hair and green eyes, he could.

He turned up his palms. "I didn't need to." He ran a gloved hand along the edge of the picnic table and scooped up a mound of snow. He shaped it into a ball. "Hans has been my eyes and ears."

She spun around. Hans stood behind her. His chin jutted out as if he was trying not to be embarrassed.

"We had to wait for the right moment to tell you." Josef smiled again.

"Tell me what, Josef?"

He turned away, tossed the snowball across the park, turned back. "Shortly after I arrived in Budapest, my parents and I were starving. We didn't have work, we didn't have money. One day I was approached by two men near the synagogue.

They bought me a few meals. I was grateful. It was the first time my belly was full since... well. We started to talk. We all agreed that the Nazis had to be defeated. They remarked that I could pass. With my looks... well, you know."

She tightened her lips.

"And well, eventually the enemy of my enemy became my friend. Not so very different than you and your Colonel Collins."

A fresh wave of anger took Lena's breath away. "Communists!" She gasped. "You are working for the Communists! All this time I have been spying for them, not the Nazis." She slipped her hands back in her pockets and felt for the gun.

Josef didn't deny it. "At first I did low level operations in and around Budapest. But when you wrote that you were working in the Physics Department at the University of Chicago... well, everyone became very excited."

Lena squeezed her eyes shut. She had mentioned her job in a letter. More than once. She remembered describing everyone in the department to him. In retrospect, how could she have been so naïve? She knew the answer. She had been in love. She had wanted to share everything with this man.

"In fact, you were responsible for my rise in the ranks, Lena. Moscow is quite specific about the intelligence they want from their American cells. They want updates on the Met Lab project. The procedures being used for U-235 separation. The method of detonation that will be used. What industrial equipment is used to test these techniques. You have access to all of it."

The anger roiling her gut curled it into a tight ball. Blood drained from her head.

"So you see, it could not have been more perfect. You fell into my hands." He looked pleased with himself. "The rest was easy."

"Easy? You lied to me. You told me I was spying for the Nazis. You forced me to go back to work after Karl—" She cut herself off. "You! You were the one who killed my husband."

He looked down. It was the first time she thought he might have felt a shred of regret. "Let's just say I let it happen."

"You excuse murder by claiming 'you let it happen?' What kind of man have you become, Josef? Why did you not ask me? Perhaps I would have..." Her voice trailed off when she noticed Josef rummage in his coat pocket. She gripped the revolver. But when his hand emerged, it was clutching a pack of cigarettes. He pulled one out, lit it with a match, and exhaled a cloud of smoke. When had he picked up that habit?

"Come, Lena. Do not be naïve. You would never have worked for us willingly."

"But why did you lie about the Nazis? Do you know what guilt—what self-loathing it caused me?"

"We had to protect ourselves. We had no idea you would turn out to be such a valuable asset. If you had been caught, we wanted your superiors to think the Germans were behind it, not us."

"So you tore apart my soul and ruined my life... for your protection."

He stiffened. "As you did mine. You left me for another man." For a moment his composure slipped and his features hardened. This was no longer the Josef she knew.

"For which you took revenge by killing him." She paused. The pieces were coming together now. "And then you kidnapped Max."

Josef's demeanor changed again, and he

resumed his civilized manner. "He is quite the young boy. I entertained him myself. Such a bright, curious child. I wish he was my son."

Lena ignored that. "And then there was Irving."

Josef blew out smoke. She inhaled the odor of stale tobacco. "He was in your way. He would have been trouble. He became what they call collateral damage."

"Collateral damage," she whispered.

He flicked the cigarette into the snow. She watched the orange tip flicker out.

"I am sorry for your pain. I was just following orders."

She tried to keep the shrillness out of her voice. "And are you following them now?"

He glanced at Hans and Dieter. "Now I make them. That is why I am here. I want to make amends. I know you are boxed in with Collins. It has become dangerous. You cannot go back to work. I want to offer you a way out. Come with me." He hesitated. "We will go to New York and disappear. I will be a father to Max."

She flinched. "But you are married. To the girl you told me about."

He smiled. "A white lie. There is no other. There

has never been anyone but you, Lena. I did this for us." He waved a hand. "Come home to me. *Hashem* has a way of balancing the scales. We can wipe away the past. Give ourselves a clean slate."

Lena recoiled at his *chutzpah*. No, not just *chutzpah*. Arrogance. Unmitigated arrogance. Was it really this easy for him to come full circle?

Josef smiled, almost as if he knew what she was thinking.

She covered her mouth with her hand. Maybe she had no other choice. He was right. She couldn't go back to Met Lab. Which meant she would have no way to support herself and Max. But if she went back to Josef, how could she survive? This man might have been her first love, but what she saw in him now frightened and disgusted her. How could he expect the past seven years to evaporate, to disappear into the fog of the past as easily as shadows grow into night? She would live in a constant state of fear, perhaps even terror. No. It was wrong. Everything was wrong.

"You used me. Manipulated me. Killed my husband. Kidnapped my son. Drove me to the edge of insanity."

"I will make it up to you. I promise." He ran his hand along the table and scooped up more snow.

She tried to suppress her revulsion. All the misery, the sorrow, and guilt was carved into the marrow of her bones. He couldn't wipe it away with a scoop of clean snow and sweet words. She wrapped her fingers around the Smith and Wesson in her pocket. "Because you want to balance the scales."

He nodded. "We are meant to be together. Ever since we promised each other in the Tiergarten. Until death do us part. Do you remember?"

She drew two steps closer. "I do. And I believe you are right. It is time to balance the scales."

He opened his arms.

"Until death do us part," she said.

Before she could change her mind, she pulled out the gun and fired. As Josef crumpled to the ground, she spun around and shot Hans. He fell backwards. She whirled around. She knew shooting two and not the third was as bad as shooting none. And Dieter was coming at her, his gun aimed at her chest. She dropped to the ground, hoping to make herself a smaller target. But it was too late. Two more shots rang out.

CHAPTER 33

Lena watched as Dieter slowly collapsed a few yards away, his blood staining the snow red. She rolled on the snow and pulled herself to a sitting position. Dazed, she touched her chest, her arms, her face. Her ears rang with the reverberation of the shots, but she was alive. And she wasn't wounded. Dieter was dead.

Gradually her ears cleared, and she heard the wail of sirens. About a dozen men swarmed across the field, most of them shouting. She watched in a detached confused state, unsure what was happening. Then, through the blur of motion, she heard a familiar voice. "Lena, are you all right? Answer me."

She tried to focus.

Agent Lanier appeared in her sightline. He ran over, crouched down, and draped his arm around her shoulder. "You're okay. Do you understand? It's over."

"I—I shot them," she whispered.

"Yes. You did."

Lanier glanced over at Josef and Hans. Lena followed his gaze. Hans lay unmoving, but Josef was writhing on the ground, moaning. Lanier's men surrounded him, blocking her view.

"Dieter was going to shoot me. How...?" She looked up at him.

"We got him first."

She blinked several times, trying to process the information. "But how did you know we were here?"

"We've been tailing you all day. Ever since you called last night. I haven't been more than a few feet away."

She licked her lips. The frigid air made them sting. "I had to do it, Terry. After what he did... to me... and Karl... and..."

Lanier cut her off. "Lena... do you realize what you've done?"

"I committed murder. Twice."

Lanier shook his head. "You have broken up one of the most important Communist espionage rings in the United States."

Her brow furrowed. "No. You don't understand. I—I..."

"Shhh." He raised a finger to his lips. "I know you're upset. You're probably in shock. But you are a hero, Lena. No one has ever done what you have. For as long as you." He took a breath. "You have been privy to the inner workings of a major spy ring. And Josef, the leader of the cell, is still alive."

Four men bent down, lifted Josef off the ground, and carried him to a waiting ambulance.

They both watched in silence. For Lena it was surreal. Then she asked, "What happens now?"

Lanier smiled. "We'll make sure his wounds heal. Then turn him, of course."

"Turn him?"

"Don't worry. You won't be involved. You've already told me everything you passed him."

"But wait." She raised her palms in a warding-off

gesture. "What about Colonel Collins? What is he going to do?"

"He's been informed. He's elated. He's calling you a true patriot."

"But I committed treason."

Lanier leaned over and offered his hand to help her up. "You were forced to. Fortunately, you came to me in time. You've been a double... no... a triple agent during a time of war for your country."

She frowned. "Are you saying you knew Hans and Josef weren't Nazis? Did you know they were Communists?"

He didn't answer for a moment. Then he hung his head. "I told you before. I've been working on this case for over a year, Lena."

"So that means yes?"

He nodded.

She dropped her hand from his. Her expression turned steely. "Why didn't you tell me?"

A pleading look came over him. "I wanted to. My superiors forbade it. They were afraid you wouldn't work as hard against the Communists as you would against the Nazis. After all, Nazis are your mortal enemies."

She gazed at him. In a way, he was no different

than Hans or Collins. He'd been manipulating her too. Using her. She should hate him. Except that he had just saved her life.

"Not telling you was wrong," Lanier went on. "We know that now. You've proven that you are willing to sacrifice your life for America. You are a star, Lena. In fact, there are a lot of people who want to shake your hand."

She stood up unsteadily. Her world had suddenly turned upside down.

"But I'll bet you just want to go home to your son."

She nodded.

"Look. I have work to do, but I'll come by as soon as I can. We have a lot to talk about." He called out to one of the men. "Archer, take the lady home, will you?" He turned back to her. "People will be talking about you for years to come, Lena."

She shook her head in confusion. "You're talking as if I am someone special. But I'm not."

He laughed. "Oh, but you're wrong. *I'm* nothing special. A normal red-blooded American. Born and bred in Iowa. *You* are remarkable."

"Normal," she repeated. Perhaps he was right. She'd been a refugee, a widow, a spy, and now, apparently, a hero. But since she'd come to America, she'd never been normal. Even though that was the only thing she'd ever wanted.

"Normal," she said. "An average American. What is that like?"

"Maybe I can help you learn." He took her elbow and guided her across the field to the car. "We can talk about that, too."

"Yes. Let's." She smiled.

THE END

Acknowledgements

Thanks go to my Street Team, especially John Bychowski, who came up with the title of this novella. And to Stark Raving Press, whose offer inspired me to write the story in the first place. I'd also like to thank the unsung heroes of my writing life: Sue Trowbridge, Miguel Ortuno, and Kristy Schnabel. I couldn't do this without you.

About the Author

Libby Fischer Hellmann writes Compulsively Readable Thrillers. Her 11th crime thriller, NOBODY'S CHILD, the 4th Georgia Davis PI novel, was released September, 2014. In 2013 Libby published HAVANA LOST, a stand-alone historical novel set largely in Cuba. She also wrote A BITTER VEIL (2012), which was set in revolutionary Iran. Her third stand-alone thriller, completing her "Revolution Trilogy" was SET THE NIGHT ON FIRE (2010), which goes back to the late Sixties in Chicago.

Libby also writes two crime series, one with hard-boiled PI Georgia Davis, the other with video producer Ellie Foreman, which Libby describes as "Desperate Housewives" meets "24."

She has been nominated twice for the Anthony

Award, once for the Agatha, twice for Foreword Reviews Thriller of the Year, and has won the Lovey Award multiple times. She lives in Chicago and claims they'll take her out feet first.

More at libbyhellmann.com.

If you enjoyed *The Incidental Spy*, would you consider leaving a review on Amazon, Goodreads, or the platform of your choice? Reviews are the "lifeblood" for authors these days, and you, the reader, have the power to make or break a book. I would be very grateful. Thanks.